The Red Queen

When Robin of Wakefield loses Blanche la Belle to Edward IV, he switches his allegiance from York to Lancaster. He allies with the Earl of Warwick and with the mysterious daughter of Henry VI. Margaret Wynford's obsession is to be awarded her royal rights. Warwick uses her to help stir Lancastrian rebellion, but this is as doomed as Margaret's love affair with Robin.

Lancaster's last hopes are extinguished at Tewkesbury field; King Henry is murdered. Only Margaret is left to lead Lancaster, though she has now inherited insanity. Jasper Tudor still crowns her Queen: Robin must kill her to save her from Yorkist revenge.

He can only buy mercy from King Edward now by agreeing to an astonishing bargain.

By the same author

THE HELL RAISERS OF WYCOMBE

FIRE AND THE SWORD

THE GOLDEN COURTESAN

SHADOW OF THE HEADSMAN

THE DOOMTOWER

WITCH OF THE WHITE HOUSE

Jane Hammond

The Red Queen

LONDON
ROBERT HALE & COMPANY

First published in Great Britain 1976

ISBN 0 7091 5297 3

Robert Hale & Company
Clerkenwell House
Clerkenwell Green
London EC1R 0HT

Printed in Great Britain by
Clarke, Doble & Brendon Ltd,
Plymouth

ONE

Like a cauldron about to come to the boil, London simmered. Sweltered in the heat of the hot August sun. About the narrow, revoltingly smelly streets, rumour flew fast and constantly: the merchant, the apprentice, the sailor and the beggar, passed it in muttered asides to one another, and shook their heads. Their womenfolk tattled at the market, and whispered at the open counters of the shops, where they thought the creaking of the sign overhead might cover their treasonous talk. For none knew these days exactly what treason was any more. When ordinary men saw the great folk of the land chop and change, with often bewildering regularity, from allegiance to the house of Lancaster to that of York, and back again; it was almost impossible to judge fairly which side it was best to be on.

For the last eight years England had known some semblance of peace. But it had always been an uneasy peace, even though it had given time for a new generation to be born who knew nothing of those bitter, bloody years of strife which had begun with the battle of St. Albans in May, 1455, and ended with that of Hexham in 1462. Edward of York had proclaimed himself King, taken Henry VI prisoner, and locked him up most securely in the Tower of London—where he still abided. A quiet, sensitive and noble kind of prisoner, for whom it was possible to feel some pity. But for the unpopularity of his wife, the ferocious and indomitable Margaret of Anjou; some gave the opinion that Henry could have held his throne against Edward's martial inroads. But Edward himself was supremely popular in London, especially amongst the women. He distributed his sexual favours with amazing fairness amongst all classes, and whilst that might arouse jealousy of their menfolk, he had their wives and daughters caught tightly in his net.

Edward! Ah, he was a true Plantagenet: overriding and arrogant. Once he had been willing to listen to advice, most especially from my lord of Warwick, but for some time now he had been showing the truth of his character, his anger at being told what to do. England now had a Queen whom most men judged deeply unworthy of him, Elizabeth Woodville, daughter of a minor country knight. Edward had married her in desperation because she alone chose to forbid him her bed; but he had married her secretly, while Warwick was making a fool out of himself trying to arrange for a wedding between Edward and Bona of Savoy, sister of the French queen. That, of course, had been the first blow. The first real souring of the relationship that had previously brought Edward, son of the Duke of York, to push his claim to the crown of England with victorious success. Without Warwick, whom men had already nicknamed "Kingmaker", Edward would probably have still been a scowling and resentful nobleman shackled to the Lancastrian court of Henry and Margaret.

It was a pity for the continued peace of England that King Edward had not stopped angering Warwick after his marriage to Elizabeth Woodville. Since that time there had been other quarrels and Warwick's brother had been deprived of the office of chancellor. My lord was not the man to endure these insults tamely. It was time for Edward to be taught a lesson. He had offered the King's brother the hand of his elder daughter Isabel, which Clarence had accepted with alacrity, very much against the King's wishes. Warwick was not to be fooled; he ordered his agents to stir up the first insurrection in years in Yorkshire and while Edward marched to quell it, Warwick attended the marriage of Isabel and Clarence at Calais.

England had trembled a little; sensed the renewal of trouble which was bound to come again soon. It had not helped for Warwick and Clarence to return home in ostensible friendship. A fresh rebellion had soon robbed the horrified Queen Elizabeth of her father, Earl Rivers, and of her brother. Warwick had been in the temporary exalted position of holding one King, Henry, in the Tower—and the other, Edward, in Middleham Castle; whilst he then promised the throne itself to Clarence.

But my lord had hoped for too much too soon. The Yorkists disliked the plan; Clarence was weak and stupid. The scowling Richard of Gloucester appealed to them no better as King. Warwick had been forced to change his tune and to make a kind of reconciliation with Edward and his queen.

Temporarily. That was what all London muttered and whispered. Temporarily. For the King could no longer trust his old friend. Warwick's bitterness against Edward and Elizabeth was not over and despite all the work of the past it went deep enough to encourage my lord Earl to think with sour interest on the apparently lost Lancastrian cause. On King Henry VI and Queen Margaret. Henry's fierce consort was in France, ever eagerly poised for any fresh chance of re-conquest no matter how placidly her husband occupied his cell in the Tower. Frenchmen had been seen skulking in a barge on the river and running hastily down the back lanes in the vicinity of Warwick's great riverside house. Frenchmen who left fine pieces of velvet torn away in the hands that had tried in vain to clutch and detain them. The visitors were noble then; rich.

And King Edward was officially unaware of their presence.

"They came to Warwick," hissed the people then, fearfully. Angrily. "It is to start again—the strife of the roses; it is to start again!"

"By the Mass, I am not for it! Cannot we live in peace?"

"The King suits me. Henry in the Tower—he's a madman. Everyone knows it."

Eyes were turned in a kind of silent awe to where the old fortress crouched menacingly over the river. Yes: Henry was a madman, even though he had never done anyone any harm. Why hadn't Edward killed him while he had the chance? Did he pity him too? Had he made the same mistake, allowing Henry to live on, so that he would furnish a jealous and spited Warwick with a real reason for new rebellion.

* * *

From Fish Street to Gracechurch Street, through Cornhill and into Cheape, paced my Lord Robin of Wakefield. Pensive-visaged, even darkly so, despite the bright hot sunshine and the vivid colours all around him: reds, blues, and verdant greens. They were splashed abundantly over the cramped, squeezed-together houses; depicted lavishly on the swaying signs of guilds and merchants. The mass of humanity hemming him in, often jostling him, was not to be outdone. Brilliant cloaks, fantastic hats, shoes that ran into ridiculously long points, that had to be held up by chains lest their wearers trip and break their necks: all the extremes of fashion were in London and affected by anyone who could afford them. Gallants—or were they merely apprentices?—pranced by, with a startling show of gaudy yellow hose on one leg, and red and yellow stripes on the other. Laughing loudly and raucously, clearly they had known more than their fill of ale from one of the numerous taverns.

Robin found himself glaring after them, he could not have been more out of tune with their mood. He came to a halt with one gloved hand resting on the chased hilt of his sword, scowling. Sweating in the heat of the sun. God's eyes, he ought to be indoors, stretched out in cool nakedness. Preferably on Blanche's couch with the fair and frail lady at his side. Frail. Ay, that was the trouble. Robin had come to like the woman far too well for his own good, even though he had always known she was fond of variety. What a fool a man made of himself when he began to dream of offering a wedding-ring to someone like Blanche, but that was the way of the world.

What had she said to him, chuckling softly, as they lay together in the darkness of last night? After he had made his magnificent proposal that she marry him and go back with him to his manor in Yorkshire?

"Fie, fie, my lordling! You speed ahead much too fast."

Too fast! They had been regularly in each other's company for at least six months, not counting the brief interlude Robin had been forced to spend away from Blanche at Edward's side during Warwick's recent insurrection. The

King himself—who had no trouble at all with women—had poked him in the ribs with a sharp elbow and jested that it was time he found himself a wife.

"For, believe me, my friend; a wife may become something of a shackle if a man is minded to tie himself too close to her, yet she is still a comfort when no other entertainment seems to promise."

Well, King Edward ought to know. Besotted as he might have been on his Elizabeth Woodville, he had given his Queen scores of reasons for jealousy since their marriage. It was very well for him: he was a king. Women lined up for his attentions. Robin had taken his dutiful share of them as a young gallant was almost expected to do, but he had never yet found one he wanted to make his wife. Except Blanche. And God damn it, she seemed ready to refuse him!

Why? What had happened? He could have previously sworn she would have been ready, even grateful, to oblige him.

A bevy of ladies passed by, giggling high and infectiously. The wives and daughters of goldsmiths he guessed; elaborately dressed in the most costly brocades, with high pointed hats from which veils drifted, set on their heads. They, too, looked as wealthy as noblewomen; in these days when so many of the old families were made poor by the Wars, they probably were better off.

Robin turned morosely to find his own tavern: to sit over his jug of ale at a broad wooden table. He paid for it with a coin flipped carelessly over at the buxom serving-girl, and remembered to give her the almost traditional pinch on the rump. If he had been in a better frame of mind it might have inspired him to suggest a more advanced encounter to the wench, but it was not so. She looked disappointed as she moved away; he supposed that was a compliment.

The church bells were ringing out for Compline, a cascade of musical sound that seemed at times to rock the city. Robin found himself stirring, brought back to the reason why there were now noticeably so many other rather watchful faces to be seen around him. Why the talk seemed often to be so low, when it was normal to hear noisy jesting and ribald roars of mirth, as the ale went steadily down. The bawds indeed seemed to be doing little but sitting about awaiting attention that was not forthcoming today.

Of course, it was this business of the Frenchmen glimpsed in the city by dead of night. London had buzzed with it all day, though Robin had been too preoccupied with his own problems to listen too hard.

He reviewed the situation now and felt uneasy.

Suppose it were true? That Warwick was seriously considering what would once have been an unimaginable switch to the almost vanquished Lancastrian cause? No one could doubt that he had the ability to carry it through if he chose—even though Margaret of Anjou was his bitterest personal enemy. Warwick was a great warrior, Robin had fought too often close to his side not to know that. At the second battle of bloody St. Albans; at Towton, and at Hexham. He had been a youth then, yet the sights he had seen on those great, trampled, gory battlefields, had soon turned him into a man. King Edward had shown him his gratitude for his support of himself, and of his brothers, Clarence and Gloucester; given him gold and extensive additions to the land Robin's own father had bequeathed to him at his death. His mother had died not long after his birth. Robin had grown up an only son, fiercely independent; closely allied to the cause of York from a very early age. He had never questioned the traditional loyalty of supporting the White Rose.

But Warwick—ah, Warwick was more interested in supporting his own cause and that of his family. Edward had been a fool to anger him, he ought to have known better. But nothing excused the conduct of the sly Kingmaker. Ay, if Robin must take up the sword anew in Edward's cause, he would turn it against his old companion-in-arms without compunction. But it was a pity to think again of war. A man reached the days of his late twenties and bethought himself of settling down.

Back, miserably, to Blanche.

What to do? How to persuade her to follow his way? By the most direct course perhaps; by paying no attention to her demurring? He had heard Edward say often enough at Westminster that most women liked being swept off their feet by a determined man. Very well then, let it be so. He would try the trick.

Robin came to his feet and strode masterfully through the throng of people in the ale-house. A few curious glances followed the tall man with his unmistakable bearing of military arrogance. On his scarlet cloak he wore the King's badge conspicuously, the golden sun of York. Respectful mutters followed him. He had been seen riding often enough in Warwick's company and in the King's.

But Robin had no thought for any of them. He was heading unerringly for the goldsmiths' shops. He knew exactly what he wanted from Master Mark, a craftsman whose skill with precious metal had already recommended him to the Palace of Westminster.

He was greeted inside the shop with low bows; Master Mark sent his apprentices out. Probably he thought Robin was on some new errand for the King.

"I greet you most warmly, my lord. What can I have the honour of serving you with today?"

Robin smiled faintly, the goldsmith's eagerness was amusing.

"Something new for Her Grace the Queen in the way of a necklace perhaps? I have several new pieces which might please her." Master Mark began fumbling in his trays, bringing out glittering chains and pendants. "This one—set with a stone blue as Her Majesty's eyes? Or this one—a beauteous ruby, my lord. There is not another to touch it in London."

"No, no." Robin waved the baubles away. "You mistake my business, master. I come on a private quest."

"I see." The goldsmith's face fell. He packed his goods away silently.

"You will not be disappointed with your fee, if you have what I want," said Robin quickly. "Bring me rings. Fine gold rings, heavy enough for a lady to feel solidly on her finger."

So that she might not forget it was there? he asked himself cynically.

Master Mark looked at him with new interest. But there was still no comment as the new goods were laid before the customer. Thoughtfully, Robin began to pick his way through them. He took his time; he wanted to make the perfect choice. Blanche had long and elegant fingers; she could wear a broad band of gold set deep with diamonds and emeralds. Ay, that was it. If Elizabeth Woodville's eyes were blue, those of his Blanche were a pale, mysterious green: emeralds for her.

"I will take this one," Robin said, pleased with his choice. "And also a collar of pearls."

Master Mark looked astonished.

"My lord means to be generous," he said at last, passing the packages over. He counted out the gold Robin gave in exchange with swift, deft hands.

My lord shrugged.

"It takes the wink of a jewel to warm a lady's heart, Master Mark."

"Ay," the goldsmith chuckled then. "And not one of them does not wax the kinder at sight of a gift. Royal or commoner, eh my lord? Good luck to you."

Nodding sagely he went back into the dark reaches of his shop and Robin emerged into the sunlight again. It was early evening now and the real heat was easing from the sun, bathing the city in a pleasant warmth instead. Nevertheless, Robin found himself sweating. From anxiety perhaps as he turned his steps towards the Aldgate quarter where he had bought himself a fine town house.

TWO

Strange: he could not open the massive front door. It must be bolted from behind. As Robin raised both fists and began to hammer violently on the thick oak, small casements opened in the houses across the street and people began to yell down abuse.

Robin felt consumed by some kind of sudden panic. What was wrong? What was going on here? Where were the servants he employed?

"Amity!" he roared. "Cecily! What in the devil's hell are you doing? Let me in! It's the master—let me in!"

"Hold your noise!" bawled a fat old woman from across the street, her red face closely bound about by the old-fashioned white wimple. "Hold your noise, whoever you are!"

A metal cup came crashing down to the cobblestones, narrowly missing Robin's head.

He sprang back, shaking a furious fist up at her window.

"Leave off, you misbegotten old cow! Mind your business!"

"My business? I'll mind it, sure enough! I'll call the watch if I have more of your row, you poxy knave!"

Robin was choking with fury, face scarlet. He was ready to leap across the narrow strip of cobblestones and go charging up to the loud-mouthed old woman, and at this moment he knew perfectly well he was so much out of control as to have struck her down with an all-too-violent hand.

He was saved from the episode. The bar across his front door was being drawn back with anxious, scraping haste; at once Robin had forgotten his slanging match and was jumping forward to push the door back, but it was still caught on its secondary defence of a massive chain and he was confronted by Blanche's white, scared face with that barrier still between them.

"Holy Mother!" bawled Robin, struck. "What's this then, woman? Am I locked out of my own house? And you looking as if new visited by a ghost?"

There seemed to be something very wrong with Blanche. Her usual poise was utterly shattered; she was trembling. He had never seen her act so oddly before.

"Robin—? You said you would be supping with my lord Hastings tonight. I did not expect you back until after Lauds."

"I changed my mind," he snapped. "Take off this chain before I hew it from the door."

"Yes, Robin, yes. To be sure."

Blanche fumbled foolishly with the hook and the heavy chain dropped to the floor with a resounding clatter. Robin hardly gave her time to stand aside before he was through into the darkly panelled hall, peering angrily up the narrow flight of steep steps that led to the upper rooms.

She stood back, following his look with real apprehension, biting at her lips.

"There's someone up there—isn't there?" he challenged her fiercely now. "Someone you don't want me to see?"

"Don't be foolish, Robin," she protested. "It is but a visiting friar."

"A friar? With the front door barred against visitors?"

He turned and seized her in a violent grip, eyes running with piercing new interest over her frightened face, her most resplendent attire. Surely he had never seen this magnificent robe of silver brocade and white fox before? That breathtaking necklace of diamonds? The extravagant horned head-dress of silver tissue framing her pale beauty; eyebrows and hairline plucked clean to lend the smoothest possible sweep to her high forehead?

"Blanche," snarled Robin, "you are at the deceiving of me again! Don't lie, woman! Don't lie! Just whom do you have up there?"

He was storming up the wooden steps two at a time, hardly even hearing her panic-stricken plea to desist. She picked up her heavy skirts and scrambled up after him, panting. By the time she gained the top, Robin had already flung open the door of the main chamber with a crash. This was an infinitely pleasant room with its warm wainscoting, its red and green tapestries, and its carpeted table. Several wide-armed chairs were strategically placed near the table, and by the huge hearth, which on this hot day had been blanked off by a big embroidered screen. The last rays of the sun were streaming in through the latticed casements, and in the brightness of them sat a brown-robed friar. Just as Blanche had told him. The figure kept very still, shoulders hunched, head bent down.

Meekness and humility? Never! Robin knew that massive form too well to be deceived. There was something like a wave of blackness, sickness mingled with shocked loathing, threatening to overwhelm him.

By the Mass, how much of a fool could a man be?

"Don't, Robin!" Blanche shrieked behind him as he

strode over to the figure and ripped off the concealing hood. At once, the mock friar straightened. Lifted his blond, all too handsome head, and stared mockingly back at his henchman. Edward the King said nothing, however. Only indulged himself at last in a faintly apologetic smile.

It was not so with Robin. Stupefied, horrified, he could still hardly believe his eyes. He was looking helplessly from Blanche back to Edward, unable to take the truth in.

"Holy Cross!" he finally yelled. "So this is the way of it! You slut!" he hurled at Blanche, and she burst into tears. "Now I see the truth! Small wonder it is that you have turned cold to me of late! You have been used to seeing better in your whore's bed!"

"Robin, no!" She flung herself at him and clutched at his arm, still weeping. "It was not like that! Believe me! I've been ever grateful for all you have done for me—I always will be!"

"Small gratitude!" he roared. "I knew there were others! I never dreamed my liege the King himself was numbered amongst them!"

"*Amongst* them?" asked the cool royal voice suddenly. The King was rising to his full, imposing height of six-feet-two. He topped Robin by a good six inches and it was more than disconcerting. So was the level gaze from the steel-blue eyes.

"I am sure you exaggerate, my lord. The King is never found *amongst* any company where ladies are concerned. They keep their devotion for him alone."

"Then for once, my liege, you have been deceived!" snarled Robin furiously. "Even as I have been! I lay with this woman myself last night! Ask her—ask the whore if it is not true? Ay," he gave a sudden, short and bitter laugh, "I persuaded myself she would become my wife! More poltroon I! See—" he dug into his pocket and threw the goldsmith's packet on to the floor with contempt. It fell amongst the rushes and Blanche stared down at it as though it terrified her. Indeed she moved back from it as if it was a snake.

The King looked somewhat shaken for the first time. He changed colour and cleared his throat.

"Wife?" he repeated. "Come now, my lord, I was not to know that."

"What difference would it have made to you?" shouted Robin. "Half the husbands in London wear horns with shameful complacency, thanks to the King!"

Edward began to look angry.

"It is not for such as myself to beg a subject's pardon. But you've served me right well in the past, Robin of Wakefield, and I regret any wrong I may have done you by borrowing your woman. It was not intentional in the beginning. I caught glimpse of her at your window, waving, and she seemed more than passing fair."

"Ay," growled Robin viciously, "I doubt it not. She would have waved her kerchief bravely enough, anxious to get you within."

"You do not sound," said Edward pointedly, "as though you have much trust of one you would wed."

"Trust? No, I have never trusted her!" vehemently. "But still I would have married her!"

"Then what prevents you?"

Edward was backing steadily towards the door.

"If I say I relinquish her? With sorrow it is true, mistress," he made a light bow the horrified Blanche's way. Her tears had ceased almost comically. "But my good friend has made his claim clear, and I stand aside for him. Even if it is for the only time in my life."

"So you have taken your pleasure and now you would go?" yelled Robin. "Leaving me graciously with my more than shop-soiled goods? No, God damn it! You can take her with you, my liege! I wouldn't have her now if she was the last woman on earth!"

He leapt upon Blanche, threw her, screaming, at the King's feet.

"There, take her! Do what you like with her! I found her almost in the gutter and made her what she is! She can eat and drink like a lady; dance and sing! In bed she is superlative; but then you know that, my liege. As you admit, I have served you well in the past. I serve you again by giving her to you—gladly! I ask only that you go from my house—both of you! Now!"

He turned his back on them and raged over to the window, banging both fists down hard on the stout sill. He heard the rustle of Edward's coarse robes, the swift step of his foot; the door opened and the King was gone down the stairs and back out into the cobbled street. Presently, Robin heard a mule clattering away.

Behind him, there was a stifled, bitter sob. Blanche, the silver robe torn under the arm and the resplendent head-dress knocked foolishly awry, was scrambling to her feet. Robin clenched his fists; he wanted to turn and slam both of them into her face, crushing it into a pulp of scarlet, black and blue. Devil's dance, why hadn't Edward taken her with him? Even if only to toss her into a bawdy house on the way?

When he turned, she was on her feet, trying to smooth out the gown with shaking hands. Her mouth looked loose and silly; her face was wet with tears, the paint on it smeared.

"You see what you have done?" she cried at him hysterically then. "You misbegotten clown! I had the King—the King!—and you have driven him away!"

"Run after him then!" roared Robin in new, white-hot madness. "Run, whore! Pursue him clean to Westminster and into the very presence chamber of the Queen! See how you will fare!"

"You!" Blanche lashed at him. "How dare you hold me up to such contempt before Edward? You had no right! No right at all, simply because I have lived with you for six months! You found me in no gutter, by God! My mother was the mistress of Duke Humphrey of Gloucester—ay, and of Cardinal Beaufort! I was brought up in a house finer than this one—slept soft and lived well until she was disgraced with Eleanor Cobham!"

"A pretty record indeed!" jeered Robin. "Much to be proud of! I seem to recall she shared my lady of Gloucester's guilt and penance, walking in her shift barefoot for the crowds to spit upon her, the lighted candle in her hand! You'll end the same way, Blanche. By the Mass, it is fitting enough! But don't look to me to help you when the day comes!"

"Look to you? I'll never do that again! I've finished with you!"

She had seen the package where it still lay amongst the rushes. Suddenly she was emboldened enough to kick it scornfully away with her toe.

"I'd rather be dead than married to you!" she screeched at him. "I'll tell you the truth: you're not half the man the King is! Not a quarter! He's worthy of any woman. But you—! You're only at your best astride a courser with a broadsword in your hand!"

This was madness. Why should words like those seem to cut the very ground from underneath his feet? Destroy him and make his knees turn to jelly so that he could almost believe that what she told him was true?

Seething, weeping with disappointed fury now, Blanche fled. She clattered down the stairs in her turn and was gone from the house, Robin could have no idea where. Neither, in this awful, dark and shattered moment, could he possibly bring himself to care.

* * *

Robin had forced himself to supper with my lord Hastings. It was a well-mannered affair, taken with ease in the candlelit small garden at the back of Hastings' house. Only the faint afterglow of daylight remained late in the sky over towards the Tower. Pinpricks of light showed through the windows of the distant fortress, and glimmered through the unshuttered lattices of the clustered houses along the river banks. Under an awning at the end of Hastings' garden, several musicians were playing and the night air was heavy with the scent of flowers.

An idyllic kind of setting, but neither my lord Hastings nor my lord Wakefield, seemed fully able to appreciate it. Their appetites were not doing justice to the elaborate courses the servants had come soft-footed to put before them, but they were consuming a surprising amount of wine.

"I wonder," said Hastings presently, eyeing his guest quizzically, "if we are troubled by the same problem?"

Robin shifted uneasily on the seat.

"I would doubt it. But I apologise for my inability to conceal it."

"Don't trouble yourself, my friend. You must see the black crow sitting upon my shoulder also. Ah—shall I whisper a name? Warwick! I am gravely worried about him. So should you be."

Robin shrugged wearily.

"Ay, well I might. I like peace well enough. But what's a man to do with peace, if he's no place to settle down in? It could be I am as well in the thick of a battle—slain even."

"Come now!" Hastings was astonished. "That is not you. You confound me. Ah, I see the way of it: it is only a woman who can be involved. Some flighty jade has led you on, and turned you down."

"As to that," grimly, "I cannot tell you the truth of it."

Hastings fell silent. He played with his meat with the tip of his jewelled knife.

"What am I to conclude from that?"

"Nothing. Or everything, as you please."

"What might be your lady's name?"

"Her name? Blanche. Blanche la Belle they call her."

"Ah, they!" swiftly. "So she is well-known about the city. Indeed, I believe I have heard of her. Did not Germaine du Bellay have a daughter by some man unknown, and try once to fob her off on Duke Humphrey of Gloucester before he was killed?"

"She is the same," said Robin with some reluctance. "She is du Bellay's child. But I never heard her try to pretend she was anything to do with Gloucester. Her mother died in the pest-house, a short while after old Henry Beaufort.

Blanche was earning her keep in the time-honoured way when I first found her: deny it though she does, her skirts were ragged at the hem, and her shoes were letting in the rain. But I had never seen a woman like her."

"At last I delve into the mysteries of your close-concealed mistress," murmured Hastings. "Many of us have wondered for some time who she was. Perhaps it is no wonder you have kept her name so quiet—it is likely to your good fortune that the wench has left you. She has a bad history. Her mother never brought anyone good luck, and neither, I suspect, will she."

"Then there are those who live more dangerously than I, who ought to beware touching her!" Robin found himself snarling. "But they do not scruple to meddle, for all that!"

Hastings had gone quiet again. The musicians had reached the end of their tune; they had chosen a bad moment. Moths came winging to the dancing candle-flames and burnt their wings, falling to the table.

Robin's hand was unsteady as he reached out again for his half-empty wine cup. He thought he had been foolish. Hastings, Edward's closest friend, could hardly have failed to note the inference. He looked taken aback though; it was obvious he had known nothing of the King's poaching.

"I think," he said at last, "you ought to regard the situation carefully. Does this not prove that the girl is poison to you? It needs real power to control her kind. Real wealth. Believe me, she will value nothing else."

"What you are telling me," gritted Robin then, "is that I could not be good enough for her."

"On the contrary, my friend. I think you demean yourself most unkindly by viewing such as marriage with her. You ought to remember that there are those others who are placed so high that none can drag them down—but that you, nor indeed myself, can ever hope to be of that kind."

"You mean the King," rapped Robin at last. "Let's have done with this foolery. Ay: it's the truth. I came back from the city today and found her with him. It near felled me. I, who have always given my best in Edward's cause, to be treated so!"

He regretted the outburst the moment it was complete, for he sensed swiftly how the previously pliable atmosphere had changed. Changed with Hastings' voice when he spoke again; smoothly superficial to Robin for the first time. Was there still some kindness lurking behind it, prompting the deceptively gentle warning?

"My lord, you surprise me. You are too hot over this matter altogether. Edward has taken away several women who pleased me. What of it? I find replacements with ease. So can you. So will you—if you are the wise man I always believed you to be."

It was no use. Robin could hold back the raging emotions no longer. He had always respected Hastings just as he had admired the King, but to be made a fool of by one, and then patronised by the other, was too much.

He jumped up and the wine spilt over the table: Hastings pulled back from the stream of it with an astonished curse.

"You ought to hear this!" Robin shouted at Hastings. "Whether or not I am wise, or a fool, is my own affair! The King has long since commanded the use of my sword, but he does not and will never command my thoughts! Sneer if you will, I was much committed to the woman. I am not going to forgive Edward for mounting her behind my back! Now you have his ear, tell him so."

"Me?" rapped Hastings. He had whitened with anger. "A

bold man speaks a challenge like that himself! Do I conclude you will not be at Westminster any longer to do so?"

"You may conclude that I shall keep to my lodgings to brood over my wrongs," Robin said sullenly, vengefully.

"Have you forgotten that this is no time for the King's loyal men to indulge in private feuds?" shouted Hastings then.

"No, my lord," bitterly. "But it does not help me. You can tell Edward that as well."

Habitual courtesy was not to be denied, yet the bow Robin made in parting was very brief and slapdash. With one hand he had snatched up his cloak and with the other his elaborate hat and he was gone from the astounded Hastings' garden before my lord could say another word.

He recovered himself swiftly. He shouted for several of his servants.

"Brock! Weston! Here, at once."

The men came running, they were tough, broad-shouldered individuals, adept at handling troublesome situations —and indeed people—if that should be necessary.

"Follow yonder lord," he instructed the men now. "I want to know everywhere he goes, and in particular everyone he meets with, in the next few days."

They nodded, grinning. This work was familiar enough. If they were surprised to be set on the track of the good-natured and loyal lord Wakefield they gave no sign of it.

"Where shall we reach you, my lord?" asked Brock.

Hastings stood up, brushing down his doublet with a kerchief. Some wine stains were still obvious on the expensive velvet. He would have to change it.

"I'm bound for the palace," he said curtly. "You shall seek me there."

THREE

For Robin, three days of mental agony. Drear loneliness. Moods of desperation interspersed with black furies, in the midst of which he leapt from the bed where he lay for most of the time, drinking, and set about tearing everything Blanche had left behind to ribbons. He pulled out her fine dresses and slashed them with his sword, trampled on her head-dresses and her veils, swept her tiny pots of cosmetic paint from the table and left them lying on the floorboards in a welter of brilliant colour and shattered fragments.

For she did not come back. An end must come to his anguished listening for a knock on the front door, or her light step back on the stairs. His servants had returned: wide-eyed with curiosity. He had sent them wrathfully away, dismissed them. He only wanted to be left alone. On the third day the heat was giving way to dull, stifling weather that promised a cataclysm of thunder to come. He opened his eyes, drawn out of exhausted sleep by the first mutterings in the darkening sky and the deadly sense of loss descended on him again at once. He seemed to remember that he had wept during the night, hands clawing uselessly into her side of the enormous bed.

It was no good. He might as well give in; she was not coming back. Ever. Hastings, God damn him, had been right. Blanche la Belle wanted better out of life than Robin of Wakefield could give.

But where in God's name had she gone? He had to find out. Suddenly his house was a prison, suffocating him. He no longer could stay here, closed in with his desolation. It was better to run out; out, even without the cover of a cloak on his back; even though the first enormous spots of rain were beginning to spit on to his window. There would be a downpour, so thick he could hardly see his way through it. He did not care. He was speeding through the streets in torrential rain that kept even the dogs sheltering; soaked to the skin and hardly aware of the giant thunderclaps creeping steadily nearer until they were over his head. Great spears of lightning shot across the black sky; the city, baked in sun for the last two weeks, steamed under the rain. Muddy, stinking puddles formed in no time in the ditches; Robin stumbled into one covering himself with filth. He retched once but then he was off again, stilll running like a madman. He could think only of finding the woman.

"Blanche!" several people heard him yelling over the noise of the storm. "Blanche!"

"That fellow's run crazed," muttered the sheltering watch to one another, letting him pass. "He'll end in the river. Good riddance."

Hastings' men, drenched and blaspheming, were not far behind. Gasping for breath, they were finally forced to a halt, they could run no more.

"Nigh three full days he keeps us waiting, kicking our heels outside his house with naught to do! And now he comes out like some devil's spirit into the storm!"

"If you take our advice, you'll let him go," grumbled the watch, praying they were not going to be ordered to join in the pursuit. "Likely the devil himself's got possession of him."

"Ay," muttered Brock at last, breathing slowing down. "Likely."

He exchanged a meaning glance with Weston. It was a good enough excuse for losing their quarry. Hastings couldn't argue with it.

The watch were beckoning them into a tavern sympathetically.

"You can't stay outside like that, masters. Come inside. A good sup of wine will warm your innards."

* * *

At Westminster, the darkness of the afternoon had caused dozens of tall candles to be kindled early. They waved their pale flames maddeningly in the thousand draughts that had suddenly sprung up with the onset of the violent storm; courtiers who had been fanning themselves for air and mopping sweating foreheads, were suddenly reaching for cloaks to stop themselves shivering. The Queen and the Princesses had been huddling together, frightened by the worst of the thunder and the tremendous roar of the rain on the steeply sloping roofs. Edward the King, his brothers Clarence and Gloucester, and Lord Hastings, were whiling away the time with the slow game of chess. They peered hard over the boards, for the light was poor.

"How do you fare with Hastings, George?" chuckled the King once. "He is a tricky player and not easily cornered."

"London is full of such men," commented Richard of Gloucester, glancing up. His gaze, dark and deeply analytical, was always disturbing. He did not care much for Hastings, and his best efforts did not always conceal the fact.

The thunder was beginning to recede; the noise of the storm grew less. As if by tacit consent, movement was breaking out again in the palace and women were sighing with relief.

Cicely, Duchess of York had come into the royal apartments, curtseying to her son the King, nodding pleasantly in the direction of his family. Still an attractive woman despite her age. In her day she had given rise to a healthy crop of scandals, thanks to that beauty. Enemies still called Edward "the son of the archer" in mocking reference to some low *amours* his mother was supposed to have indulged in at Rouen, while his dead father was Regent of France.

But Duchess Cicely was such a proud woman it was difficult to believe it of her. She had been far from pleased to see Edward marrying the comparatively inferior wife he had chosen. Relations between her and Elizabeth were not always cordial. Neither did she feel over-amiable to the Duchess of Bedford; Jacquetta of Luxembourg.

The Queen had risen from her chair with relief.

"Thank the Holy Mother," she said, "that clamour be done."

She looked enormous, her shape incredibly distorted by the latest royal child the King had begotten. Her own blonde, fragile beauty, appeared faded with tiredness.

"The storm," said Duchess Cicely too sweetly, "is sure to return."

"I take that unkindly," said Elizabeth at once, frankly indignant.

The King was sighing, pushing away his game. Clarence and Hastings followed suit, watching. Edward was turning in an unusual, faint irritation on his womenfolk.

"Ladies, no squabbling, I command it. Madame my wife,

madame my mother—be peaceful."

"Your pardon, my liege," dared Duchess Jacquetta, "it is hard for my daughter to keep herself subdued when she is goaded on by those who should know better! She carries the heir of York in her womb. She must be treasured."

Duchess Cicely exploded.

"The heir of York, madame? Let us hope so! The Queen has given my son three children already—all girls! We seem to be waiting a long while for a Prince!"

Elizabeth shrieked and covered her eyes, bursting into tears; the little Princesses Elizabeth, Mary and Cicely promptly followed suit. The King jumped up, furious; Clarence and Hastings retreated. Richard of Gloucester, wearing a look of inexpressible boredom, took the opportunity to leave the scene.

"I will not tell you again!" shouted Edward. "This is not a market-place, nor you a gaggle of fishwives! Leave us, my ladies of York and Bedford—leave us! Take the Princesses with you!"

He was very conscious indeed that Elizabeth Woodville had to be treasured: he did not need Duchess Jacquetta to remind him of that. Perhaps some of her initial allure had worn off now, and perhaps much of that had been encouraged by her unattainability as a mistress, but he was still devoted to her. So long as she did not expect him to be even transiently faithful.

He went to the Queen and put a reassuring arm around her shoulders; the weeping slackened.

"Here now," said Edward, "dry those tears. The world is wet enough without them today."

He was grinning down at her, forcing an answering smile.

"Summon the servants to bring in food for void," he told

her, "I hunger."

She nodded and went ponderously away to order the trays of cakes and sweetmeats to be brought in. Edward sat down again, shaking his gold-maned head.

"Women," he grumbled good-naturedly. "They give so much pleasure, and arouse such anger. They ought always to be treated lightly, but alas, they will not have it so."

Hastings smiled, perhaps a little remotely. It was ironic that, at that moment, he should catch sight of Brock and Weston hovering agitatedly behind the stalwart King's guards standing at the entrance to the royal apartments. Brock waved his hand urgently and Hastings at once leapt to his feet.

"Your pardon, my liege," he said to Edward. "But I think we have the news we have been waiting for."

"Ah!" Edward was different now, sharp and attentive. "Comes it by those fellows? By all means let them enter in."

Brock and Weston looked overwhelmed as they came into the sumptuous room. The tapestries, the furniture, the display of gold and silver plate was clearly intimidating. And the magnificent figure of the King himself in his fine crimson doublet and breeches, the glittering collar high around his neck.

"Greetings, masters," the King said in an attempt to be reassuring. "Lord Hastings' servants are always welcome in the palace."

"Sire—my lord—" they looked nervously towards Hastings. "We have to tell you that the man you charged us to follow has escaped us. In the storm; but none could have held him. He ran from his house to God knows where. He could have been snatched up by some fiend of the lightning for all we know."

"Fools!" said Hastings angrily but Edward touched his arm forbiddingly, still staring at the men.

"Is it your opinion that he is then demented?" asked the King.

They shrugged. They were supremely uncomfortable both with their setting and with the dampness of their clothes.

Edward grunted and sat down. His conscience was troubling him over Robin of Wakefield. They had been good companions-in-arms so often; Robin was a trusted and reliable friend. Had he not sent him often on his private errands since peace had come? To make purchases for him in the city, to take word to his various women? Indeed, he knew that was how Robin had first seen Blanche la Belle—in the house of the goldsmith's wife, Jane Shore. How could the King have guessed the fool would become so enamoured of the pretty whore he had already made use of before Robin had taken her away? Only as a light amusement; he had almost forgotten her when she waved to him as he passed by in procession. It was really a pity he had given in to impulse and sought her out again; by lying with her anew he had aroused a veritable hornets' nest. Wakefield had kept her identity so secret it had almost been laughable, but it was no laughing matter now. His grudge went much too deep. Edward had already given him time to come back to Westminster and make his peace: if he had done that, he would have told him that the girl had come running to the palace, and that he had graciously consented that she should take a place within, as one of the chambermaids to my lady of York. Indeed, Wakefield the repentant could have had her back.

But what now? Wakefield was not repentant. It did not

look as though he was ever going to be.

"You swear the party did not move from his lodging until now?" demanded Hastings.

"Not a step, my lord."

"Hastings," said Edward, "stop. You will not convince me that a man like that will be driven to what is in your mind."

"Your pardon, my liege. But I believe you wrong. You cannot take such a risk with this tension about the city. Warwick has not been near you for a week; he is too busy with his own nefarious business."

"So," growled Edward in reluctant assent. "God's eyes, that's true."

"Sire, whether Wakefield has simply run mad with grief or whether he is nursing thoughts of treachery, he is no longer of worth to you."

"But——"

"Sire, give me leave to act."

"I like it not," protested Edward.

"It is necessary, Sire. My men must seek Wakefield out again if it is possible, and then he must be slain. For your own protection. You could not take him back."

The Queen was returning with a number of servants trudging behind her. They bore platters of light food. Edward looked towards the sweet cakes and his mouth watered.

"Ay, be done with it, then," he snapped at Hastings. "But I don't want details. Just say that he is dead, and add no more."

Hastings, his eyes gleaming with relief, bowed. He waved a commanding hand at Brock and Weston and took them out. The silent, rather worried-looking Clarence, followed them. Well he might be deep in unease, wed against his royal brother's will to Isabel Neville. It had of course been his intention to keep a foot in the Warwick and Edward camps, if he was not exactly a traitor yet he was as close to being one as he dared.

But Clarence would survive. The good ex-companion Wakefield must pay the price and die.

"What business has been sitting so low on Hastings' brow?" asked the Queen keenly. She had become accustomed to smelling out trouble that involved women. Her every sense was alerted by inward warning now. Besides she had already caught sight of a particularly beautiful young woman newly taken into the service of the Duchess of York, her mother-in-law.

"None to trouble you, sweeting."

Ay, she had thought as much. That was Edward's fobbing-off voice.

"What can have happened to my lord of Wakefield?" murmured Elizabeth. "I have looked in vain for him about the court. Jest says he is sick of love."

"Jest?" Edward could not keep the sudden harshness out of his tone. She thought his blue eyes looked momentarily haunted, but the look soon vanished. "It's no jest. Hastings has found out that he is a traitor."

Elizabeth gasped. The colour drained from her face.

"Never! Not he! I think nothing could drive him to that, except——"

Her voice trailed away. Edward seemed foolishly embarrassed; she really needed to say no more. She was angry, filled with sudden contempt. She rose to her feet and swept her black velvet skirt to one side imperiously. Her high head-dress glimmered in the candlelight, the small coronet around it flashed with gems.

"I hope you can rest easy on thoughts of your own perfidy, my lord! Ay, and that you can forget spilling Wakefield's blood while you lie beside your new whore! It always pleased you best to take another man's woman. One day you will reap your own reward!"

Furious, she rustled away.

It was a pity Edward had had the commonsense to foist that girl on Cicely of York. If only he had bestowed her on Jacquetta of Bedford, both Elizabeth and her mother would have enjoyed making Blanche's life a misery.

FOUR

Robin had fled until exhaustion finally overcame him, and he found himself hurtling to the cobbled roadway, to lie there panting and spent. For a while the rain had battered its force on to his inert body, but in a way it was almost welcome for the way it streamed down his sweating face and back. When it eased he found he could raise his head again. The terrible clamour in his brain was receding, the beginnings of a new, more coherent reasoning was possible.

The storm and his mental agonies had burst upon him together; now he knew the violence was spent. He pulled himself up slowly, clutching on the wall. For a while he hung there, waiting for the curious weakness to abate. His clothes ran with water; his hair was plastered to his face. He must have been a wild sight enough, he thought, one to terrify any onlooker. Somehow, he must make his way back to his own part of the city, to the house. He could face it again now. At last he had fought to accept the inevitable absence of Blanche. But he had not forgiven Edward.

Was it that knowledge that made him suddenly turn to look up at the grey walls against which he had been leaning? High they were, stalwart. Surrounding one of the fine riverside properties of the nobility, the gardens of which sloped clean down to the Thames. He could hear birds beginning to sing in the trees within as the rain stopped. The city in these brief moments was strangely silent: folk still nervous to take the first peek out of doors in the wake of the storm.

Robin was shivering. But not only with cold, there was a strange excitement at the back of it too. For he knew where he had run, all unaware. This was Warwick's house; the rear of the Kingmaker's great London mansion. This small, iron-studded gate would be the one out of which the mysterious French were said to have slipped, earlier in the week.

There was not a soul to be seen. But there was a large empty keyhole in the door. He knew that by bending to peer through that hole he would see the mysterious places beyond and it was totally irresistible. Robin crouched down, applying one eye to the small aperture. He had been right: green vistas of lawn met his eye, banks of beaten-down flowers and a great grove of trees growing almost down to the river's edge. And Warwick's house. Massive, grey, with twisted chimneys and slanting roofs, silhouetted against the still leaden skies.

He was so engrossed, he did not hear the clatter of hooves until it was too late. He jumped back from the gate in the most guilty haste as a richly curtained horse-litter lurched and bumped its way along the narrow lane. It had outriders; one of them spurred forward immediately, shouting, sword upraised.

"By Heaven, what knave's this?"

Robin had time to see Warwick's device of a bear and ragged staff emblazoned across the man's tunic before he was pinioned against the gate with the tip of a broadsword at his throat. But the emblem on the other outrider's chest was completely unknown to him: a cluster of white daisies on a field of gleaming black, with a border of gold fleur-de-lys.

"Run him through!" cried this man, his voice high in agitation. "Run him through! He's a Yorkist spy!"

Surely it was the shortest time ago that Robin of Wakefield would have yelled furiously back that he was right, and be damned to him? Not now. The full-throated denial was immediate, and made without the slightest compunction.

"Wait, masters! Wait! It's not so, I swear it by Our Lady!"

The litter had come to a swaying halt. As Robin stared towards it with faintly glazed eyes, the heavy curtains suddenly parted.

"Leave him!" commanded a musical, feminine voice. "Leave him. I command you!"

She was peering out, this mysterious woman who kept herself so carefully concealed. The two guards were grumbling, drawing back but to their astonishment, Robin made no attempt to flee. He could not. He felt rooted to the spot by the vision of such beauty in a face, pale, almost madonna-like in its serenity. The lady had large, thick-fringed and totally bewitching hazel eyes; the hair looped up under her fantastic horned head-dress was a burnished copper. Her nobility was unquestionable; the big diamond studs on the furred bodice of her sage velvet gown, the heavy gold collar round her elegant neck, even the mass of rings on her long fingers, told him that. But there was more: she had an air about her even from a distance that made Robin feel he ought to bend the knee to her, honour her like a princess.

"Who are you?" she was demanding. "I have bidden the men spare you. Now what is your name, and why do you peer through my lord of Warwick's gate?"

Robin pulled himself up and approached her, darting a glare at the still angry guards. At once she moved back, waving a forbidding hand at him.

"Not too close!"

"I beg your pardon, lady," he said almost humbly and bowed. "I do not mean to frighten you."

"I am not easily frightened," she replied with asperity. "I merely wish you to keep your distance."

"Very well," said Robin. "But you asked for explanations I was about to give."

Perhaps it was the faint ring of irritation that persisted in returning to his voice even in this situation, that made the unknown lady look towards him with increased interest.

"You're a bold fellow," she accused him. "And the more so with your life so newly spared."

"I thank you for it, my lady. With all my heart."

"Your name?" she insisted again.

"Madam, I fear that if I give it, your men will not be swayed even by your command from running me through."

Astonishingly, the curtain was opened further. She beckoned him. He thought he glimpsed a transient fear in her beautiful eyes, and he was puzzled as to its source. Yet she did not retract, only continued to recline on her silken cushions and watch him. As he drew near some warmly intoxicating fragrance drifted over him from her person; he felt himself trembling a little. A strange sensation, very new to him. A most pleasant one. It was a shock to glimpse a thick band of gold on her wedding finger, but of course he should have been prepared for that. He guessed her to be all of Blanche's age.

"Now," she said, "speak your name softly. I won't betray you."

"Why not?" he asked. Bewilderment struggled with mockery. The undoubted danger of his situation was not entirely able to overcome his startlingly keen sudden interest in this superlative woman. By the Mass, had he really thought Blanche the fairest in the world? Had he really suffered so much over her? "Why should you not betray me if you think I am an enemy?"

"You know nothing of me," she said quietly. "Let us talk instead of my lord of Warwick."

"Very well. I am Robin, lord of Wakefield. Does that answer you?"

She caught her breath. The hazel eyes glimmered.

"Ay, right well. Then you are not simply my lord's enemy, but a mortal one."

"And therefore yours?"

"Perhaps," softly, "perhaps."

"I—could not hurt you," he told her frankly.

"I believe you."

"I meant no harm to the Earl of Warwick."

"Of that I am not so sure. But go from here now and no more shall be said. Have no fear: I shall not tell my men who you are."

"Your generosity leaves me speechless, lady."

"I conclude nevertheless that it is a state foreign to you," she smiled. The whole of her lovely face seemed to glow with animation. She held out her long and elegant white hand to him. He took it almost reverently and dared to touch it with his lips.

God's eyes, she let it linger in his much longer than she should have, before she drew it gently away.

"Go now," she said. "Go. You will not look upon me again."

"Is that why you are so kind to me?" fiercely.

"Step aside, Robin of Wakefield. Just take your life and go. And tell King Edward nothing of the lady of the white daisies. You understand?"

A bargain for a bargain. That was fair. Except that she could have no idea that Robin had not the slightest intention of returning to King Edward again. Once betrayed was once too many: even though he had seen a woman more than Blanche's equal at last. Was she not just as unattainable? Could he not witness that for himself?

He stood out of the litter's way. She had closed the curtains again and the guards were hammering loudly on the gate. It was opened quickly from within; the first outrider who bore the lady's arms on his tunic, took the plodding lead-horses inside to the grounds of my lord of Warwick. In no time she was gone and the gate had been slammed massively shut again on the outside world.

* * *

Who was she? Who? Wending his way back to his house in a kind of daze, Robin could think of nothing else. White daisies! What ought he to remember about white daisies? He knew there was something important and intriguing about the emblem which was escaping his memory.

The storm had circled London and it was coming back. The birds were retreating anew from the skies and sheltering under the sloping eaves of the crazily leaning wooden houses. Robin quickened his step. He had no mind to be caught outside in another torrent of rain. Yet the mysterious and noble lady had clearly been glad enough of the previous storm, for it had enabled her to make entry to the city with scarce a soul about the streets to see her.

Why then was it so important that she should not be seen? There could be no doubt that if Robin had still been the King's friend, he should have run to Westminster with the news at once: this was of far greater significance surely than visiting Frenchmen? Or were the two events connected?

In God's name, what was Warwick about, scheming and planning in that house by the river?

Robin was so engrossed in private conjecture, that he had no inkling whatsoever of new danger. He turned the corner, hastening in the increasing downpour. A new fork of lightning lit up the black sky over St. Paul's; the thunder rolled. At the same moment Brock and Weston had jumped on him, daggers ready in their hands. Neither of them had really believed he would come back, but they must not let Hastings down this time; they were determined to make the most of their luck.

Gasping, struggling, the three men had fallen to the ground. Robin strove to free himself; he was strong and experienced in a fight. One knee crashed into Brock's chest and sent him choking back, the other fist had somehow found a mark on Weston's chin. Before they could reach again for their daggers, Robin was back on his feet drawing his sword. Without compunction he plunged it deep into the first man's back as he struggled to get to his feet; Brock screamed faintly and fell back. Weston had scrambled up, his own sword now at the ready. Back to the wall; Robin fought him off; the blades crashed and rang; they stalked each other, clothes and hair running again with the wet, feet slipping perilously on the cobbles. A sudden thrust, a parry. Weston out of breath, scarlet in the face.

This was Robin's moment: he sprang forward beating down Weston's failing guard with a welter of massive blows, the man stood no chance now. His last scream rang out as he saw the swordpoint delving straight for his defenceless chest with no escape possible; but the sound of it was lost in the overhead clap of thunder. Like Brock he was slithering to the ground to die in a pool of spreading blood.

Panting himself now, Robin bent to wipe his blade on the man's black cloak. Still holding it in his hand he sped on his way back to his house. For the moment he had forgotten the mysterious woman; he was too confounded as he realised that Hastings had set his men on him, bent on assassination.

The front door was still open as he had left it. He slammed it shut and leaned against it, getting his breath. Then he barred it and put up the chain.

Hastings! So the feud was mutual now. Royal. Hastings never did anything without Edward's consent. Westminster had decided my lord of Wakefield was a potential traitor, even after the years of service he had given to the White Rose.

Robin trudged up the stairs. It was only four days since he had come home to find Blanche with the King: it seemed like eternity. In those four days his world had been turned upside down, and then right side up again so often that he felt dizzy and sick.

In God's name, what now?

He went over to the wine jug, almost dragging his feet with sudden tiredness, poured himself out a large measure of the red liquid and fell into a chair. This was a sorry mess and no mistake. Now he appeared to have no place to go. He would be slain if he went back to seek out Edward, if not in the palace then probably *en route*. He should have asked himself this question before: how could a man live safely in London as a Yorkist if he was not the friend of the King?

Had Blanche really been worth all this trouble?

"It's no use," growled Robin to himself. "I'll not pardon Edward for his wrong, whether she was worth it or not. I loved her."

Loved. Was he really using the past tense and having some real hope of having meant it? He rose from the chair and found himself scrabbling down on his knees, searching for the package he had brought for her with such high hope. He did not really know what he wanted it for, but suddenly he had to find it.

The rushes were dirty and beginning to smell but he brushed through them with anxious determination. At last he found what he sought, still wrapped up in crumpled packaging. He tore that off and stared at the beautiful, heavy ring in his palm. Green emeralds for the pale hue of Blanche's eyes. By the Mass, they would suit another lady equally well—better.

You fool, Robin told himself. You saw the kind of rings she wore already. Worth twice the price of this one.

No matter. He stood up, brushing himself down; he slipped the ring into his pocket. He was going to regard it as some kind of good luck charm. Luck—by God, he needed plenty of that.

Robin's face had taken on a curious grimness. He went to strip off his soaking, filthy clothes, to pour out water from the pitcher to wash himself. He did so with a particular care, almost as if cleansing himself from an old way of life, ready to begin anew.

When he was finished he went to the clothes chest and took out fresh raiment: good velvet and brocade, a feathered cap with a fine ruby brooch pinned on the front, long leather boots. He owed none of this to Edward, it had been purchased with money from his own estates.

The storm had finally gone, leaving only a drizzle behind it. But it would be dark early tonight. Robin sought in the chest for one other article: a long black cloak with a hood which could be pulled up over the cap. He would need such concealment. Had Hastings' men not made that obvious?

You cannot do this that you plan, his mind urged him. It is against everything you have ever been taught; or believed in. You will get no happiness out of it, for your conscience will never rest. A grudge against Edward cannot make you into a Lancastrian overnight; you have never been an opportunist turncoat. And why should Warwick want you? Why should he trust you? He will likely set his men to kill you, just as Hastings did.

Yet the fact remained: where else did he have to go now but to the enemy camp? Edward obviously believed him capable of it. He might as well lie guilty dead as innocent.

Besides, how could Robin deny the lure of that mysterious door in Warwick's wall, the one through which the copper-haired enchantress had passed.

No doubt that she was for Lancaster.

Might that not be reason enough to follow her way?

FIVE

Richard Neville, Earl of Warwick, sat alone in his private apartments. Surrounded by the luxury he loved and cherished. A tough, broad-shouldered man into his middle years long since, a warrior of enormous repute who also liked to bedeck his person with the utmost splendour. The cost of his clothes and his possessions was the least of Warwick's worries; he was one of the richest men in England—and they were growing sparser these days. Several long-established family fortunes had already petered out under the grinding financial pressure of endless civil war and battles. Not Warwick's. He had always ridden high on the waves; he still rode high. "Kingmaker" men had christened him, and he enjoyed the title proudly. After all, it almost sounded like King itself. He was the uncrowned King. Without his power and support Edward would have been nothing as Henry was now. And Edward had shown himself undeserving of Warwick's magnanimous service again and again, starting with that appalling marriage to Lord Grey's widow, for which Warwick would never pardon him, though he had kept on careful good terms with Queen Elizabeth at least until this last year. Now he told himself such ploys would no longer matter. They must realise at Westminster that he was at some deep game of his own and the jest of the matter was that none of them knew how to stop him.

They couldn't even get King Henry slain and out of the way if they wanted to with Warwick standing between the Lancastrian monarch and the Yorkists. Squarely. And if Edward had offended, Henry had done nothing at all. He was a quiet, shy and ever-forgiving man, caught up in his prayers and private penances. Warwick should have reviewed all this before, realised that if he must rule England through a puppet—and the people would not permit anything else—Henry was the easier choice. He could be made to dance to Warwick's tune where Edward would either demur, or these days refuse. Or go behind Warwick's back and try to scotch his scheming from there.

Clarence was not much better. Warwick, by marrying his daughter Isabel to Edward's brother, had thought to buy himself a very useful adherent. He had made a mistake. Clarence was weak. Jealous of his brothers, but weak. Although his wife was a Neville he was not showing powerful enough sign of being ready to betray his brother permanently.

No. Warwick had paced this room endlessly in the last months, trying to make up his mind over the same kind of problems that had bedevilled Robin of Wakefield. York or Lancaster, which was it now to be?

He had begun making preparations soon after Edward had taken up the crown officially again. He had sent careful, courteous messages off to France, addressed to the King, Louis XI. Margaret of Anjou was living in the isolated country château of Kuerere in Verdun, with her son Prince Edward and a scattering of loyal Lancastrian servants. Louis XI had received her very coolly into his lands after her last flight from England, for it was said the Queen did not have a great deal of money. Only, no doubt, the caustic and iron pride with which Warwick had clashed all too often in the past. In the throne-room, in the council-chamber and even on the battlefield, for the turbulent Queen had not been afraid to don armour and ride out with her husband and her son at the head of her armies. Much good it had done her, forsooth.

But never mind. Here was a promising turn to her fortunes, if she but knew it. Or if Warwick could possibly encourage Louis XI sufficiently to begin to make the Earl look even a little less like Queen Margaret's sworn and deadly foe. For this, Warwick knew, would be the sticking point in his new plans. On Margaret of Anjou's acceptance of him as her new ally, everything rested. There was cause therefore for a worried frown on Warwick's face tonight as he sat quietly and drank Hippocras out of a gemmed goblet. There was no avoiding facts. Louis had sent messengers to him in secret in this last week and the news they had brought had not been good: Queen Margaret still hated him with venom.

By God's head, she had always been her own worst enemy. She had learnt nothing, for all she liked to boast she could think like a man. She was wrong. A man who wanted everything had to learn to swallow old bitternesses and quarrels: force them to the back of his mind under the expediency of today.

Was it really possible she might still change? He had already taken an unprecedented step to try to force her hand, one which would certainly astonish her; which might shake the fierce woman into a new train of thought. If it did not, then King Henry VI was likely to rot away the rest of his life in the Tower, and Warwick would be left without the powerful weapons he needed so much now to teach Edward a lesson. He was pleased to think of the unease that must be in the King's mind. He must know that Warwick was no longer his friend, even though it had suited him to pretend that he still was. He would know that plotting was going on, but he was unable to stop it because he had no proof—and because the Earl was too strong for him.

A servant was discreetly tapping at the door.

"Enter," called Warwick, pulling himself out of his meditation. "What's amiss?"

The question came sharply because he could see confusion on his man's face.

"Nothing, my lord. It is not troublesome. Merely that a tall fellow swathed in a dark cloak has been taken, lurking within the grounds. Apprehended and questioned he demanded to speak to you. He says it is of importance. I think he is of no account. Shall he be thrown into the cell next the river?"

Warwick frowned; drummed his fingers briefly on the table.

"No," he decided finally. "I'll see him. If only to demand how he came within the grounds with the gates fast locked."

"He says he scaled the walls, my lord."

"The devil he does! Then he's mighty agile and strong. Bring him in."

He sat back to await the man's arrival. There was no doubt of his approach by the scuffling and cursing, and the scraping of feet that presently arose in the corridor. Two of his most stalwart men dragged the unknown visitor inside Warwick's chamber and forced him to the floor.

At once the Earl was on his feet, striding over to the group and ripping back the hood. Robin's fine array was more than a little pulled about by his climbing and then rough handling, but despite it he thought he had done well enough to get this far, still with his life preserved.

Warwick looked struck.

"By Our Lady!" he ejaculated. "No wonder you kept yourself concealed, my lord!"

"Only that I might reach you!" Robin shouted quickly, seeing Warwick's hand creep to his jewelled dagger. "Don't judge too fast, my lord Earl. I have not come here as an enemy."

"Then how?" snarled Warwick.

"Out of curiosity," said Robin, knowing he must be interesting now or perish.

"Curiosity!"

The Earl seemed confounded; the idea had worked. He put away his dagger.

"What kind of talk is that? Do you come from the King or not?"

"If you will allow us to be private, my lord? There is, pardon me, something I must know for sure of you."

Warwick had paled. Relations with Edward were still untrammelled on the surface, what did all this mean? His shock was pushing him into being careless. Ever since this all-too loyal Yorkist had been dragged in to him, he had spoken as though he was already on the other side. Or had the man been clever enough to prise that reaction out of him?

Warwick strove to calm himself. He even attempted a cold smile and waved the servants away.

When they had gone, Robin rose from his knees. Warwick stared at him, then re-seated himself at the table, gesturing to another chair.

"No need to stand, my lord of Wakefield," he said. "Come, I take you at your word. Make plain what your curiosity is. Or is it the King's?"

"I have been well enough known as Edward's messenger." Warwick could not miss the bitterness and at once he lifted one eyebrow. "But I'm here on my own business. It may be the end of me. That's for you to decide."

"Me?"

"It very much depends on whether you are the King's man or not, my lord. Some hope you still are; some are convinced that you are not. I will be straight with you. I was his friend. I don't need to say that. But I am his friend no longer."

A strange silence had fallen. It was quiet enough almost to hear the sand sifting steadily through the hour-glass. Warwick was watching him with fiercely glinting eyes.

"Now let me understand you," he said softly at last. "For you are asking for some mighty confidences. Ones which I could well be not prepared to give. How would I know you are not a trickster, sent by Edward to smell me out? That is," meaningly, "if there was ought to smell out?"

"My lord Earl, I fear I have brought nothing with me that can convince you. I am left begging for your trust. Except that if you wait but for morning light it is likely you will hear that servants of Lord Hastings have been slain near to my lodging."

"And your sword bears the guilt?" swiftly. That was obviously different; Warwick looked changed, attentive. "But Hastings, too, was your ally."

"Of course he was, my lord. But the King, knowing my wrath against him, gave him permission to set his ruffians on me. Now do you see how I stand?"

Warwick leaned forward.

"I would still need to know what were the grounds of your quarrel with the King!"

"My lord," Robin sighed wearily, "a woman. She I would have made my wife."

"Ah!" said Warwick with evident satisfaction. "Now that I can believe."

He had visibly relaxed. He lifted the magnificent wine jug and poured a measure of the good Hippocras out, offering it to Robin, who took it gratefully, drinking it down.

"Some might say you have made an undue fuss about one who was clear enough a whore," he said. "You must have known that of her yourself."

"I did."

"Then you were a fool. You have a noble name, Robin of Wakefield. Why besmirch it? Would you ever have been sure the sons she bore you, were your own?"

Robin shrugged.

"She is gone. It is no matter now."

"Except that Edward has lost his friend."

"Ay, my lord. He has lost him. And his friend seeks a new place to offer his services. That is why he comes to the Earl of Warwick and asks him plainly if he knows of one."

Warwick grunted. He rose and began to pace slowly round the room, the expensive damask of his long gown rustling over the rushes. A massive gold chain hung round his neck, his belt was set with rubies. His heavy, lived-in face was frowning again, almost sombre.

"If he did," said the Earl at last, "he could but recommend it with reluctance at present."

"But—"

"Now hear me!" Warwick rounded on Robin suddenly. "Mark this: whatever the rumours that are fast flying round the city, there is no immediate hope of freeing King Henry from the Tower. No hope of any battle to oust Edward. She who is the essential rallying-point for such resistance, is not only driven from England—but is more than unwilling to trust new friends. Who, alas, mean only well by her."

"Margaret of Anjou," said Robin. "Ay, I see it."

The rank feud between the Queen and the Earl was common gossip, and had been for a decade and more. Likely Warwick would find it almost impossible to patch the utterly threadbare relationship up—even with the promises he might be making.

"If I could help," Robin ventured, "consider me very much at your service. Consider me a very willing convert to the cause of the Red Rose. There, I can say no more. I have declared myself a traitor to the King, and am in your power if you wish it so."

"Magnanimous," smiled Warwick thinly. But no responsive declaration was forthcoming as yet, he was too clever for that. "Wait here," he told Robin, heading for the door to call his man back. "There is no need to tarry until morning to test you. If you have been sent here as a spy Edward will not expect any move from me yet. I warn you, however, if you have been lying to me, your corpse will be thrown into the river before dawn."

He went out. Robin could hardly prevent a sensation of unease as the door was barred behind him and he was left a prisoner. Suppose Hastings' men had already been discovered by the watch and dragged away? Where would his proof be then?

Ah well, if he must die, he must. But why should he, when he was still young and strong? He was excited despite himself by the brief hint Warwick had given of the intrigue that was going on with France. Amazing. Two weeks ago he could never have believed that he would would ever be able to look at the Lancastrian cause with anything else but contempt, or view its personages with anything else but scorn. Yet it had only taken the falseness of one woman and the bewitching hazel eyes of another to change him, modify him, teach him tolerance. Robin had never had time for turncoats. Was this some lesson he was supposed to learn?

He went poking curiously about the room, peering behind tapestries, lifting the heavy hangings over the windows to stare out into the black night. No moon; the city across the river was shadowed deep. Southwark. Blanche and her mother must have known much of Southwark in the past, for Warwick was right, they had been prostitutes both. Robin moved away. He fingered gold dishes and ornaments, went so far as to help himself to more wine.

Where, he wondered eagerly, had the woman in the litter gone? Was she still somewhere in this great fortified house, hiding away under Warwick's protection? It had been very obvious that she had not wanted to be seen arriving.

Who *was* she? What could be her connection with the Kingmaker?

He found no answers about Warwick's room. Only waited in increasing impatience for over an hour, until the door was finally unbarred again. There was a mutter of voices and then Warwick himself came back inside. Robin came nervously to his feet despite himself. He thought he must have paled.

Warwick waved him back to the chair. He closed the door and went over to the table, unlocking the casket Robin had previously observed there.

"My lord Earl?" he queried finally, unable to bear the suspense any longer.

Warwick was sifting through papers. He lifted one out, scanned it, then came back to Robin with it still in his hand.

"The men were found," he said briefly. "Brock and Weston. I knew their faces well. You have involved yourself in a rare little turmoil, my friend."

He was holding the document out for Robin to take and read. With a slightly shaking hand, the lord of Wakefield took it from him and complied. The first thing that struck him was the royal seal of France appended to the edge of it.

"Louis XI, the Most Christian King of the French, to his noble friend Richard Neville, Earl of Warwick. Whereas it has much pleased us to attempt the first reconciliations between the lady Margaret of Anjou, Queen of England, and yourself my lord, it is regrettably my task to inform you that the said right noble lady will as yet have none of you. Not the utmost of my protestations will move her at this time; but I have not given up hope. Surely it is the lady's dearest dream that she shall be restored with our brother, King Henry VI, to their rightful throne of England. I believe she will accept you, my lord of Warwick, if you give her further proofs of your change of heart."

Robin looked up. He thought Warwick was very shrewd. He had still made no confession of his treachery by word of mouth. But this told the story ably enough.

Robin gave the letter back.

"I understand how you did not recommend the cause, my lord," he commented gravely. "I can only repeat my offer to help. It is the same as it was before you left me to seek Hastings' men."

"Ay," said Warwick curtly. "Ay. But don't run away with the idea that this is some kind of chivalrous adventure, Wakefield. There's much to be done. Persuasions to be added to mine, likely some Yorkist blood to be spilt."

"I am eager enough for your purpose."

"No doubt. But are you also discreet? Devious?"

"I can be, if that is what you want of me."

Warwick gave a short laugh.

"You will find Queen Margaret a hard mistress to serve. She gives nothing and takes all. White daisies—ha! Never had a woman more unsuitable an emblem!"

"Daisies!" repeated Robin, thunderstruck. "God's eyes!"

"Ay, what's amiss?" asked Warwick sharply, not understanding the confusion. Why should he, when he knew nothing of Robin's chance encounter with the beauteous female outside his gate?

White Daisies! Of course, that was it: that was what Robin's fuddled brain had been trying to remind him of, from the first moment she had mentioned the flowers. Yet—what sense did this make? If white daisies were the emblem of Queen Margaret, what was the other lady doing, making claim to them—causing them to be displayed so extravagantly as her own arms? Only some relative would dare; indeed, even the closest relative might do so. No wonder then, that he thought her bearing more than royal?

Warwick was frowning at him keenly. He was no fool.

"I think you know something," he accused Robin now.

"Something, I ought to warn you, that might be more than dangerous."

Robin shrugged finally. Helplessly.

"I saw her," he said at last. "The one who came here earlier. The fairest face I ever witnessed, despite the one who betrayed me. She told me herself that King Edward would give much to hear of her presence, but I never would have told him. Even if I had still been his man."

"So," said Warwick heavily. Almost sombrely.

He sat down as though some great weight rested on his shoulders and made him suddenly weary.

"As long as I live," he said, "I shall continue to be confounded by the twists and turnings of womens' minds. You say this—lady—spoke to you? Went so far as to confide such facts to you? It is hard to believe. Ah but—" as Robin protested, "I feel it is right that I should believe you."

"Is she still here?" Robin found himself asking with eagerness. "I would fain pay my respects anew."

"She is gone," snapped Warwick. "As the first darkness fell: her business here completed. You ought to forget about her."

"I cannot," said Robin simply. "And I hope that in serving you, and King Henry, I shall also be serving her."

"Small doubt of it," said Warwick grimly. "So you're smitten, that's the truth of it. Take my advice: take your slighted affections elsewhere in haste. That one is utterly beyond you—and married, withal."

"My lord of Warwick," earnestly, "do you accept my sword in the Lancastrian cause?"

Warwick hesitated only a brief while.

"Ay," he agreed. "I will do so, God help me. I have need of strong men like you. You must know much about the

Yorkist camp; more than myself, for I have kept myself something apart from Westminster of late."

"As I pledge you all that, I ask you to tell me that lady's name. As a measure of confidence, my lord; as proof that you trust me."

"By the Mass, you're a bold fellow," growled Warwick. "I warn you, you are better off for being in ignorance. Few, indeed, know the truth of her. Queen Margaret herself will be angered with you for it. Does that not give you some clue? Also her business here? I have been brought to try all manner of ploys to try to bring that woman round to my way of thinking: letters, bribes. From those she respects and those of her blood."

Understanding was indeed beginning to come. Mind-bending it might be; for Robin realised he had come upon the closest-kept state secret since the murder of Duke Humphrey of Gloucester. But there was no denying it.

"She is the Queen's daughter," marvelled Robin.

"Ay," grunted Warwick, eyeing him narrowly. "And the King's. That's right; she is no bastard but a true Princess of England. Born during those years when everyone thought the Queen was barren, and thus she is the elder sister of Edward, Prince of Wales."

"But why—why conceal her birth like that? Spirit her off to some country wet-nurse when the realm was crying out for a royal child?"

"Because she was a girl, my lord. Frail and sickly and given to fits much too like those of her father, the King. England needed a healthy boy not an ailing maid: the Queen was ashamed of her."

"But she is superlative! Magnificent!"

"They were not to know how she would grow. She was

married off young to Richard, Earl of Wynford, and she is still his wife."

"Wynford was said not to have a wife."

"That was part of the price he paid for being given a royal Princess. Only when she died was the truth to come out and leave him free to marry officially. A very rich man for his efforts, of course."

"I think the whole arrangement vile, and a disgrace to the royal crown!" Robin found himself shouting.

It was Warwick's turn to shrug.

"Perhaps. But she has given Wynford no children, my lord. He, too, has his cross to bear."

"He must have hoped she would perish young in child-bed," said Robin bitterly. "A pretty use indeed to make of a girl between them all. And she outdid them: she grew strong and healthy. She has lived a prisoner for nothing—is that not the truth? Moreover you now mean to use her to add her persuasions to yours so her mother will accept you. She would be more than justified to refuse!"

"She did refuse," said Warwick shortly. "In no uncertain manner. By God, her hair is as red as her mother's was gold, but they are like enough in temper I promise you."

The germ of a hectic, wild idea was stirring in Robin's brain. He caught his own breath with the audacity of it, but it still drove him on.

"Let me ask her again!" he was reckless; willing to risk everything on this one throw, even if Warwick changed his mind because of it and called the guards in to kill him off. "My lord, let me go after the lady. Decry it how you will, I know she will listen to me. Else she would not have spoken to me as she did when her men caught me peering through your gate. Is it not worth the attempt at least?"

The attempt at what? To creep inside the Earl of Wynford's secret, hidden household and try to reach the heart of a woman who must have been frozen by ill-will and lack of love, all her life?

He knew Warwick saw through his scheming all too well.

"You make a fool of yourself," he sneered suddenly. "I neglected to tell you that the lady Margaret has an excellent marriage, notwithstanding its vicissitudes. And she knows her own station. You have no chance."

"Try me! If I fail to bring her to your way of thinking, I am expendable. If she will not come to mine—or indeed if she does—what does it matter to you? Is Wynford your friend?"

Warwick stirred: he stood up. He leaned a hand nonchalantly on his dagger hilt and smiled at last, very coldly.

"You ought to know better than that, my lord. I play violent games. I cannot afford to have friends. Only movable allies. I accept your offer and to Wynford you shall go."

SIX

The Countess had ridden out early, unafraid of the cooler, blustery weather which had come on the heels of the storms and remained now for over a week. Sometimes silver, sometimes grey and even threatening black, the clouds persisted in blowing past the sun and throwing enormous shadows over the rolling green countryside. Sometimes the distant Welsh mountains seemed to glisten, sometimes they glowered. How long would it be before the peaks would be seen to be snow-capped again? Time sped by so swiftly. By the Mass, and to what real purpose?

The was the question Margaret Wynford found herself putting again and again, the question to which she received no real answer. A woman was expected, probably rightly, to accept her lot in life. To make the best of whatever had been given her. Should she in fact be so ready to thresh in the bonds which had held her fast since she was thirteen? Almost a child? At the time she had been glad of release from the endless round of Welsh and border castles which had held her existence as a safe secret from all but the very privileged few. To be established at the great fortified castle of Wynford as its mistress. But she had not realised how ill a bargain it was really to be. That her world must continue to be so enclosed. Why had her mother, the Queen, continued to be so stubborn about admitting that she had a daughter as well as a son? What had the first error mattered after Edward's birth? Except that Queen Margaret could never bear to be found out in duplicity, nor put in the wrong, there was no reason at all. Margaret had long had much sympathy with the husband who obviously loved her and obeyed the rules of the royal bargain without outward complaint. What he privately thought, she paid him the compliment of believing favourable to her. Often enough she had written to her mother and begged to be recognised, for Wynford's sake, if not for her own. Always from Queen Margaret an icy silence.

The Countess wondered miserably if my lord of Warwick had any real clue in his mind as to the real source of her reluctance to further entreat her mother to make him her friend. How did he think she could turn the Queen to him? She, a daughter who had never been acknowledged and, thanks to the civil war, probably never would be. Margaret suffered from deprivation of maternal affection. Despite the Queen's treatment of her, she still desperately wished to become on good and reasonable terms with her. It was only normal; only right. But it was hopeless.

Everything was hopeless. Even now, while Margaret's laugh rang out boldly in answer to the accompanying Earl of Pembroke's jest, her heart could not have been more averse to merriment. The small mounted party had reined in, and the escort jingled to a halt behind them.

"Now then, lady," said Jasper Tudor in his deep, musically Welsh voice, "unhood the hawk. I've made you a fair wager she will not beat mine."

"My lord of Pembroke, you are a scoundrel and you know it!"

"Who succeeds these days, my lady, without being

one?" he chuckled, teasing her. Jasper Tudor knew her well: so did his elder brother Edmund, Earl of Richmond. To these half-brothers of King Henry had been entrusted much of the care of the frail little princess who had grown into so astonishing a beauty. The Earl of Richmond was at present with her mother in France, Jasper was risking his neck by a brief stay in Edward's England. He was too bold and audacious to care very much about that. Margaret often thought that he must be very like his father, Owen Tudor, who had stolen the heart of another princess, Catherine the Fair of France. Her grandmother. Maybe it was from the lovely Valois that Margaret had taken her looks, though her colouring was all Plantagenet. She was vain she supposed, but she did not allow it to worry her; she had few enough pleasures but the decking of her person and admiring her own face. It harmed no one.

She had stripped off the velvet hood with quick fingers and loosed the bird into the sky; in a trice Jasper Tudor had followed suit and both hawks were soaring up into the air, wings spread, balancing on the wind. They hovered there, almost stationary.

"By God it seems neither of us will win, my lord uncle," quipped Margaret.

"We shall see! Give them time!"

One of the hawks had seen something. Suddenly it began to plunge back towards the fields, claws outstretched.

"Mine!" cried Margaret in triumph, shaken out of her lethargy despite herself. "Mine, I tell you!"

Tudor's was following suit but it was too late. Margaret set spur to her mare and went galloping off, cloak streaming in the wind, hood falling back from her tight, glistening coif. More of her almost strident laughter came drifting back as the others thundered after her; she waved back to them mockingly. She reined in and swung down from the saddle, stooping to pick up the bloodied carcase of a hare which she held high for Tudor to see.

"You owe me a hundred marks, my lord!"

The following party reined in, Jasper Tudor shaking his head ruefully.

"Ay, I see it's your day, my lady. Well good luck to you for all that. I'll pay up cheerfully."

He tossed her a little leather bag which she caught deftly in her heavily ringed hands. That done, he saw the shadowed look return to her beautiful face; the mild diversion had lost its charm. She tossed the hare down to the dogs without another glance and re-mounted, turning the head of the mare back towards the foothills where the massive walls and towers of Wynford waited. She chose a slow trot now. Tudor watched her keenly but she seemed to try to keep a look of remoteness about her as if she did not want to be questioned.

A man did not have to be wise to see that she was deeply unhappy. That Wynford, for all it was her only home, had become like a prison to her. What had caused it? Surely not that brief, abortive visit to London which would have been unheard of so short a while ago? Only Warwick's gigantic influence had made it possible. And if she had gone to him, hoping to find some final release from her problems, she herself had refused to carry the scheme through. But returned, infinitely more restless and on edge than she had ever been before. Tudor decided there must be some hidden reason and he was more than intrigued by it.

He began to test her gently, even as the walls of the castle drew steadily closer.

"Margaret—" he had lowered his voice and drawn his mount near to hers— "what happened in the city that you did not speak of?"

By the way her hand tensed on the reins he knew he had guessed aright. But what surprised him was the faintest pink flush that arose on her cheeks. God's eyes, from another he would immediately have pin-pointed the advent of some interesting male into the scene. Now was that really possible?

"Margaret, tell me the truth. You know I would not yield up your confidence."

"I pray you," she said in a low tone to match his own, "don't speak like this further. There was nothing that might trouble you. Or my lord."

It was a man sure enough. Or she would not have instinctively brought Wynford's name into it, the unmistakable air of faint guilt about her. Tudor was dumbfounded and disturbed. This, he thought, was all that had been needed to set this cauldron simmering: the danger signs a more than uneasily based marriage could do without. For although there was no doubt that the Earl had always loved his wife, she had never returned him more than affection. Deep affection maybe, but it was not going to stand the onslaught of her falling in love with someone else.

"You have never given me cause to doubt your common sense," the Earl of Pembroke was saying slowly.

She darted him a strange look.

"I have never in my life been presented with the cause," she told him. "Rest easy. What ill can come at me within Wynford?"

It was almost a sneer for a moment. It left him feeling even more uneasy than the traces of her inner guilt.

* * *

Robin, lord of Wakefield, had now travelled in the wake of the Countess for upwards of a week. Despite the fact that he journeyed alone, his progress had been slow; the countryside was relatively unfamiliar to him. he had lodged by turn at Gloucester, Hereford and Worcester, and at last had struck off towards the Marches. He was tired but an inner spirit still seemed to drive him on. He did not even begrudge donning Warwick's badge of the bear and ragged staff for all to see. Where was the Princess Margaret now? Surely she had long since reached the shelter of her husband's domicile again. What kind of a fool was Robin to keep believing that he could get her out of it? That he had made a plan she would find irresistible, one even Warwick had not thought to try on her? But he was not going to give in. Those gleaming hazel eyes had not belonged to a meek woman, ever content to sit at home and weave. No. Had not Warwick himself given a hint of her highly charged temperament?

Therefore on the morning Robin finally reined his weary courser in, to sit gazing in excitement across the rolling fields to the grey soaring pile of Wynford, he was conscious of nothing so much as power. Of a new lift come to his life which he could not have dreamed of during those agonised days alone in London. He supposed he had done some praying for release; the prayers had surely been answered.

He did not rest long. He set off towards the castle, a

small, lost looking figure crossing the massive arena of rolling green and brown. Dwarfed by distance, yet his appearance set the garrison of Wynford into rapid activity. Some of the warning shouts reached down to Robin; he understood them. That the castle behaved as it would in time of war was not surprising when it held tightly such a person as the precious lady Margaret. With Wynford, it must always have been so. Even before the Wars of the Roses had commenced in earnest in May '55. How young she must have been then, little more than a child. She must be aching for freedom by now.

Robin kept calm as the expected troop of men-at-arms came riding out to surround him. They were tough and surly with him; they went so far as to deprive him of his sword. The serjeant was rough in his handling, only then did Robin push him away with a swift spark of warning in his eyes.

"I don't question your right to caution," he said with a meaning chill, "but there's no need to forget that some are your betters."

The man glared at him momentarily, his weatherbeaten and bearded face enclosed entirely in his helmet. Robin had already noted that these soldiers bore no sign of the white daisies about them: their patron's device was more familiar to him, a coiled golden serpent on a field of crimson.

"Take me to my lord Earl Richard of Wynford," ordered Robin sharply. "I bring word from my lord Earl of Warwick."

It made a difference at once; the surliness became far less marked. The serjeant backed away, he went so far as to nod to his men to return the sword.

"You should have spoken up sooner, master messenger,"

he grunted. "Not come creeping up without proper escort and banner."

"My business makes it unwise to have either," snapped Robin then, self-confidence that had served Edward so well over the years coming back to his manner almost without his being conscious of it. "And I am not master messenger. I am my lord Robin of Wakefield to you."

"I ask your pardon, my lord," grunted the serjeant, subdued at last. "Be so good as to ride with us into the castle. The Earl will be told of your arrival with haste."

"That's better," said Robin. "That's better. Let it be so."

Seen at close quarters, Wynford was intimidating. The castle was large and concentric; Robin guessed it had been one of those raised up by Edward I during his years of subduing the Marches and the Welsh. Round towers stood sentinel at strategic positions around the thick curtain walls; machicolations reached over the battlements to ensure those walls could not be scaled with success. The moat was dug wide and deep; the drawbridge and portcullis housed in a vast gatehouse. Nor was that all: on passing through the first portcullis, another two gateways confronted Robin, each separated by a cobbled inner bailey. Only after passing through the last portcullis, stared at on all sides by the throngs of men-at-arms pacing the courtyards and patrolling the walls on high wooden platforms, did Robin glimpse anything like the real living-quarters of this massive border fortress. He could see the Earl of Wynford's golden-serpent standard flying high over the old keep which still stood at the centre of the later works, but it was not in there the family would live. Instead Robin could see a fair expanse of relatively new building enclosed in the protection, of the impregnable shell. Built of gleaming golden stone, with traceried windows, very redolent of ecclesiastical architecture. In fact, very beautiful to behold, with a green sward of garden before it on which peacocks paraded, and where masses of small red roses grew.

He thought: it could not be more applicable. The Duchess of Wynford reminds me far more of a red rose than of her mother's flower. He wondered why she had chosen it. It must surely be a sign that she was desperate for Margaret of Anjou's withheld affection, not simply for her acknowledgment. Or had it simply been as a mark of defiance to cause the ignorant—such as Robin had been—to stare and wonder?

Robin was given little time for further conjecture. Before he could be marched up to the imposing entrance, two men had emerged from the door and stood looking at him. The one Robin knew well, he had fought on opposite sides to him for too long not to know. Jasper Tudor, Earl of Pembroke, sworn enemy of the Yorkists. His dark face wore a look of utter astonishment and it was clear from his manner of dress that he had returned from the tilt within the hour.

The other man stood taller. He was imposing, wearing a full suit of plate armour, the helmet with its waving yellow plume tucked under his arm; his thinning hair also was yellow, his blue eyes very piercing and keen. Richard of Wynford: it must be. By God, he looked formidable. Enough for a second to make a man hesitate over his purpose of trying to steal away his wife from under his nose, for whatever purpose. There would be only one way to do it: first Wynford would have to be drawn to Robin's side and made to see the merits of his plan.

But it was Jasper Tudor who was striding forward. Jabbing a finger at the badge on Robin's cloak.

"By the Mass, it seems to me that this has taken a change, my lord! I find it very hard to trust your new colours. I recall your old ones all too well!"

Robin stood his ground.

"Richard Neville did not seem to have the same difficulty," he said coolly. "And neither should you, my lord Earl. What you see is right enough. I am no longer for York but for Lancaster. All you have to do is to try me."

Tudor seemed dumbstruck. Richard Wynford was coming forward, intense curiosity on his handsome face, rather than fear or distrust. He stared at Robin fixedly.

"I do not seem to have seen you before," he said.

"This is the lord of Wakefield!" Tudor told him angrily. "Ask him how many good Lancastrians he has slain since St. Albans! Ask him!"

"I don't need to do so," said Wynford quietly. "I see he's a stalwart enough fellow."

"My lord Earl," Robin dared to ignore Jasper Tudor and addressed himself straight to Wynford, "my business is very urgent."

"If you come hot from London on the very heels of my wife then it must be," smoothly. The scrutiny deepened. Robin knew he was being tested for knowledge anew. "For the Countess spoke with the Earl less than a fortnight ago."

"My lord, let me speak to you. Warwick is greatly put out by the answers the Countess gave him on a certain matter."

"Ah!"

There was no mistake: Wynford actually looked pleased. He exchanged a meaning glance with Tudor and Jasper himself looked not without interest now, despite his distrust of the visitor.

"I thought that would be the way of it," said Wynford. "Come within, my lord of Wakefield. You will want wine and food after your long journey. After that you might be pleased to join my lord of Pembroke and myself in the tilt-yard where we are busied. We can talk there."

Wynford's constable had come out, bowing. He ushered Robin before him into the coolly luxurious hall, where my lord spent some time staring about him in awe. Warwick had hinted at the riches Wynford had earned himself by marrying the King's daughter; here was the evidence. Velvets, tapestries, fine furniture, embroidered chairs and hassocks clustered around the vast fireplace. A wide stone staircase led up to the galleries overhead where he could see doors set under archways; more rich velvet hangings and gold plate ranged along the panelled walls.

Private rooms for everyone? Wynford was modern in concept indeed. Even the hall seemed to have lost its traditional role as the great feasting place: doubtless the Earl had some vast apartments upstairs which served such a purpose now. Or did he dare do little such entertaining on a vast scale?

Wynford and Tudor had disappeared to leave him alone to his welcome meal. He was glad to have the opportunity to appreciate his surroundings and put the indefinable atmosphere of this magnificent place to the test. Two dogs joined him in due course and he threw down some scraps of meat to the rushes for them; he sawed through the good white bread energetically with his knife and chewed a slice with enthusiasm.

He could not fathom why he had the persistent feeling of prickling down the back of his neck: the real sensation of unease in so peaceful a setting. Had he been accepted a little too readily inside? Was there something he was unaware of?

Robin finished his wine. He pushed the plate and cup away and came to his feet; it was no good, he could bear this strange suspense no longer. He was being watched: he knew it.

He felt angry. He stood with arms akimbo and stared around him, only to be greeted by blankness. By tapestries hanging from floor to ceiling that shivered a little in unseen draughts. By darkly curtained alcoves towards which he began to stride, one by one, snatching back the hangings to peer inside. He didn't know what to expect: the sudden thrust of a dagger into his chest, or a blade into his back.

"Who's there?" he bawled finally, cheated.

The place must be crawling with servants and adherents of the Earl of Wynford, and yet he might have been totally alone in the entire domestic quarters of the castle.

"Who's there?" yelled Robin again. "I demand to know!"

The rustle of a damask gown on the stone stairs brought him round with a jolt, hand springing to the hilt of his sword. But despite his purpose here, the vision that confronted him was the last one he expected at this taut moment, welcome though his clamouring senses might soon start telling him it was.

This time, however, it did not seem that the copper-haired beauty was ready to share in any of his pleasure. She hung back there in the shadows, face white and angry, from the tip of her steeple head-dress to the trailing fur hem of her gown, she looked to be seething with shock and even insulted pride.

"What in God's name are you doing here?" choked Margaret. "How did you come to seek me out?"

Her voice vibrated with fury. Robin, shattered, could find nothing to say. He did not understand that his arrival into her enclosed world was like a thunderclap. That the fight she had already put up to force herself to remain here in safe keeping as Wynford's wife had exhausted her. The last person she wanted to see was the man whose existence she had only lately found it necessary to deny forthrightly to Jasper Tudor. A man whose good looks had somehow made an impression on her which was perhaps understandable, considering the almost convent-like seclusion of her life. Moreover she thought she must guess why he had come here: that it was yet another ploy of Warwick's.

"Lady—" Robin started to say hoarsely. "Lady, I—"

He remembered he was in the presence of a princess. He went down on his knees. She greeted the knowledge that he had been told who she was with a quick hiss of breath, a clench of her hands.

"Look upon me," he entreated suddenly. "Changed from the White Rose to the Red. In your royal father's name, lady, in that of your noble mother, don't despise me."

"Despise you?" she cried at him bitterly. "No! I will not think of you further at all! Go away—go back to Warwick if he really is your master now! Tell him Margaret Wynford will not change her mind! Ever! He can look for other scriveners for his letters and that's an end of it!"

She turned and ran violently back up to the gallery; he heard her speed along to the rooms which must overlook the green courtyard and the roses, and the door slammed behind her.

Robin stood gaping after her like a fool. He would not have known what further to say to her just then even if she had remained. He felt as if she had just dashed her hand across his cheek with some stinging blow. If he had any sense he supposed he would obey her and disappear now, without even speaking to Wynford for a second time.

But he was beginning to learn that where the Countess Margaret was concerned he was not going to have very much sense ever again.

* * *

Behind the tapestries, the Earl of Wynford and Jasper Tudor had moved back, finished with straining their eyes through the holes cut into the fabric. In the hall the newly arrived personage did not usually guess that he was spied upon because the chinks were cut cleverly into the eyes of the mythical gods featured there. Wakefield had proved himself more sensitive than most, throwing out his challenge to the unseen witnesses he had guessed were somewhere there.

Now of course he would be persuaded that it was the Countess who had been spying on him.

The Earl was very quiet, fingering his chin.

Jasper Tudor watched him.

"I knew," he said at last. "I knew she had spoken with someone who had disturbed her. Send him away. Or better still, slay him."

"No."

"He means trouble."

"No. I can cope with him. At least this proves he is speaking the truth. He is for Warwick and for Lancaster."

"You don't need him!"

"I think," steadily, "that we do. I want my wife acknowledged. I believe I want that more than anything else and always have done. She has the chance to seek her mother's approbation at a time when the Queen is weaker than she has ever been. To use it to plead with Margaret to trust Warwick. How else is Lancaster ever to get back the crown unless the Queen moves? And how am I ever to have a wife until the Queen will call her daughter?"

Jasper Tudor shook his head.

"She ought to be permitted to take her own decisions."

"You think he has some influence upon her? Is that not it?" swiftly. "Very well say I, let him use it. I tell you I have no fear of him. She is a loyal woman."

Pembroke wanted to say curtly that she was foremost a woman and a very lonely one. But he gave in and reluctantly held his peace.

SEVEN

Foolish it might be, but Warwick was feeling inspirited. Like Robin's, his confidence had unaccountably returned. He did not know why he should feel inwardly so sure that he was going to win Queen Margaret's goodwill after all, just because Wakefield had come out of the blue to assist him. Nevertheless, there was no denying that it looked like a real stroke of luck.

Was it time then to be stronger? To show his hand more plainly? He had nothing to lose and everything to gain. Margaret of Anjou watched England like a hawk, she would be mollified by evidence of any uprising against Edward.

Warwick called in messengers and sent them off to Lincoln with urgent directions for the score of adherents he had in the district. Then he tried something even more daring: he despatched a message to the Duke of Clarence at Westminster.

"Son-in-law, you favour our poor house so little with your presence. I grieve for it. I am very anxious to know how fate fares with you?"

* * *

Clarence read his letter swiftly. Then he crumpled it up into a ball hastily and threw it onto the blazing logs. What was the old fox up to now? Warwick never became friendly unless he wanted something. The Earl was full of promises where Duke George of Clarence was concerned, that was the trouble. Twice before he had told him he would make him King of England and he had not kept his word. Was this to be another trick?

His wife, the lady Isabel, saw that her father's message had reached the right quarter. The Duke seemed reluctant to talk about it.

"Shall you go to my father?" she asked at last.

"I don't know," muttered Clarence shiftily. "I am considering it."

* * *

Edward watched the Clarences enter the royal audience chamber together, bowing and smiling affably from left to right. A totally untrustworthy pair, thought the King. And God's body, if they were not busy with some new secret, he was not himself crowned. Clarence could never conceal his thoughts of trickery and Duchess Isabel was finding it hard to conceal an air of triumph.

The King felt justifiably uneasy, but without evidence he had no way to probe at his brother. Of course it was quite different when he reviewed the affair of Robin of Wakefield.

Edward leaned over and beckoned to Hastings. As usual this was something of a family gathering with the young princesses squabbling over a game on the floor; the Duchesses of York and Bedford sniping at each other and Queen Elizabeth half-asleep in her chair. No one was paying very much attention to the musicians; there was far too much noise.

"Now my lord Chamberlain, I've cause indeed to worry. You have still given me no news of that rogue Wakefield."

"My liege, there is none."

"None at all?"

"He seems to have vanished into thin air. I begin to think he has somehow fled the country. He must have guessed how it was with us once he recognised my men." Hastings sighed. "By the Mass, it's a pity right enough. That a man could be so much of a fool over a whore."

"She has her merits," said Edward wryly, biting into a grape.

"No doubt, lord King, no doubt. But she has caused me indirectly a very great deal of trouble."

"But she's passing fair for all that," murmured the King nodding over to the window. "She graces the court."

Hastings frowned. It was she sure enough, blondely beautiful in a grey-blue brocade, tinsel embroidered. Her exaggerated horned head-dress sparkled with jewels. A gift from the King? Ay, well he was welcome to her. And by his hints he was making every effort to enjoy her. No wonder Blanche looked heavy-eyed, seated quietly behind her mistress the Duchess of Bedford. No wonder the Queen darted her an occasional glance of venom.

"Sire, do I continue to search London for Wakefield?" asked Hastings.

Edward shook his head slowly.

"No. But I'll wager he's not fled the land. He's found friends somewhere. New ones and that is what worries me. That, and the look of mischief I see on my beloved brother George's face."

"Arrest him," urged Hastings.

"Too late," said Edward. "It would not help."

He was gazing around him strangely as though he was trying to pin-point the scene on his brain, as though it was something he knew he was going to be glad to remember once it was all swept away. Eight years of peace: how quickly they had passed. He almost did not want to put on his armour again and take up his broadsword to ride forth against Lancaster.

Edward of York had no choice. His hand was about to be forced.

* * *

At Wynford, relationships simmered. The situation was a baffling one, and up to the present time it was unrewarding as Robin had not expected. Jasper Tudor's dislike and distrust did not surprise him; Margaret's did. If indeed those were the twin emotions ruling her consistent, now icy refusal, to have any more to do with him than was forced upon her by necessity. She was a totally different person from the one he had met by chance in London. There were moments when he was brought to wondering if he had really understood the right of her there at all and if his blasé assurances to Warwick that he could steer her by his influence had not been ill-judged and highly premature.

The most he could get out of her was a distant nod of acknowledgement as she took her place at her husband's table. A glance of calculated disinterest thrown his way if he tried to edge near enough to make conversation.

"I want to make this clear to you, my lord," she deigned to say once. "You are here as my husband's guest. Courtesy forbids me to do other than suffer you but it does not demand that I show you any greater favour than that."

It was quite appalling to realise that those words almost wounded him as much as Blanche's final rejection had. But not quite. In those moments, Robin had thought he saw a wildness, a longing, hidden not efficiently enough behind the frigid mask. He was right to believe she ached for freedom, even if not for him. Was that the mistake he had made? Had he wounded her pride by following her here, perhaps making her believe that he had summed her up as an easy sexual prize?

What did the Earl of Wynford think of all this? He was indeed almost as puzzling in his own way as his wife. His friendship seemed easy to come by once the first strangeness had worn off. Not for Richard Wynford the scowls and growls of Jasper Tudor. In no time he appeared to be ready for an almost back-slapping intimacy with Robin. He began to hawk in his company, to seek competition from him at the butts and in the tilt-yard. The Earl found himself with a predictably worthwhile opponent, for Robin drew a good long-bow and handled a courser and a lance more than well.

"Excellent work!" he would call out cheerfully to see himself regularly beaten even at his favourite sports. "Excellent fellow, my lord! I swear I learn much from the observing of you."

The sun had been shining down on the patch of green where they had been standing, shooting their arrows repeatedly at the butts. But a sudden shadow had crossed the grass; it put Robin off and the next shot went wide. Or had it been the first, veiled inference to come out of Wynford that he was by no means fooled as to the basic feeling behind Robin's purpose. It did not help for him to raise his eyes abruptly to see the Countess watching them from outside the gallery. She looked different, her glorious hair bound loosely back and held in a snood. She looked younger.

"You compliment me too soon, my lord Earl," said Robin ruefully.

"Not so."

Wynford was fitting another arrow to his long-bow and drawing back the gut in his gloved hand. Although he was staring with narrowed eyes towards the target, he gave the impression that he was by no means totally engaged upon it.

"I think you are altogether a most capable man. Of course every man is liable to a mistake. Now you consider my wife——"

The arrow had sprung free; it whistled unerringly through the air and hit squarely into the centre of the gold.

Wynford straightened with satisfaction.

"She needs help. Guidance. I thought Warwick sent you here for that purpose. Of course it is not your fault if you find yourself besotted on her—"

"My lord Earl!" protested Robin hotly. His guilt must look gigantic.

"Why should you apologise? She is a most beauteous woman. Virtuous too."

That must be a challenge.

"I ought to leave here," said Robin angrily. "It is plain I serve no purpose."

"Indeed you will not! You will take your courage in both hands and confront my lady as you planned to do. You demean your own capacities by your reluctance to fight her—whatever the reason is! Come, my lord, how much longer must I stand by while you allow the frozen glances of a woman to frighten you? Go to her; force yourself on her attention, I give you full leave for it. I tell you plainly I have already spoken my mind to her about this business with Warwick but she remains obstinate. I would be grateful for anyone to move her—anyone!"

Robin stared at him speechlessly. How deep the worm of discontent had eaten into the Earl of Wynford was obvious at last. He might indeed love his wife but he was a mighty weary man waiting for her to be given her rights. Did he really trust her as he made out he did? Or was he simply so desperate that he would risk anything on any reckless throw?

"Well?" he was demanding. "Are you going to earn your keep from Warwick?"

Robin threw down his long-bow, flung the quiver of arrows from his shoulder.

"Ay, my lord Earl!" he retorted at last. "Since you give me a challenge equal to that of the butts or the tilt! You're right. I've wasted far too much time. I'll waste it no more."

* * *

Margaret saw him stride away from her husband, saw him heading with long, determined steps into the castle. The look of ruthless determination about him told her what his errand was even before she heard his footsteps clumping with authority towards her. She edged back, panic overwhelming her. She knew she was cornered; there was no way to flee, stare around in desperation though she might.

He was standing in front of her in the narrow, traceried gallery, staring at her.

"Go away!" she cried at him fiercely. "Go! I told you I wanted none of you!"

"Lady—" Robin's voice tended to quiver—"I've been more than patient. Even your husband has found occasion to tell me so! You knew why I came here—you must know, in God's name, what can be done to your own advantage!"

"I am weary of begging for it!" Margaret cried suddenly. "It is useless! Don't you all understand that?"

Her first fright was becoming intermingled with stormy bewilderment. Richard had sent him? Richard, who ought to guess how his lonely wife's heart was being entangled more each day by the sight of this handsome and persistent stranger? Yes, she had fought him. Bitterly. Why not? Why not strive her utmost to hold the mounting emotions sternly in check because they were wrong, unworthy of her marriage and unworthy of her birthright? Fine thoughts: fine prevaricating. Nothing removed the leap of excitement at the sound of his voice in the distance, the ring of his laugh at Richard's jesting. Lct Jasper Tudor scowl on; it was no good. Margaret, Princess of England, had fallen in love and she had known it was so from that first day when she had glimpsed the Yorkist Wakefield from her litter. Wakefield who had used the most shattering audacity to pursue her to Wynford itself, so greatly she had impressed him. God damn him for it. God damn the joyous triumph that kept threatening her because of it.

"My husband, you say!"

She actually laughed at him, hard and contemptuously. She was a good actress, she told herself. Incredibly good.

"Ask him yourself, lady, if you doubt me! He is more than anxious to see you reconciled with your mother. It is not so very unworthy of him."

Margaret's bewilderment was complete. God's eyes, so after all there was to be no word of love coming out then?

No hint? And she was the one who was continuing to suggest by her attitude that such a climate prevailed?

She went scarlet; she turned away. Such a thing was quite unthinkable.

"Lady—" Robin's voice had softened, he could not help it. Driven by anger as he had been, even embarrassed by Wynford's hints, he had found the ability to be unkind and ungracious at last. Very well, he knew it had been needful. But he still loved her and it still hurt him to make some kind of a fool out of her. She would be brought to resent it furiously. He would have to take that chance. He dared not be too gentle now, at least the success of his mission might be in sight. "Lady, you told Warwick that the written word was useless between your lady mother and yourself."

Her back tensed visibly.

"I put it to you, Countess Margaret, that if you were to choose to confront the Queen yourself, it would be different. She has never seen you grown. Is that not so?"

The silence was complete. It almost vibrated with emotion.

"My lady? Are you considering what I speak of? I want to tell you that I am most ready—if you wish it—to take you to France."

When she finally spoke her voice sounded low and hoarse.

"And you have reason to think my husband will even agree to such as that?"

"I think he will agree to anything, lady. Anything that will free him from the bondage you share without entailing your death."

"I have thought of that," she said suddenly. Bitterly. "Is it not well that my lord loves me?"

She rounded on him with a swiftness that caught him unawares. He was shocked at the change in her: the fire in her magnificent eyes and the heightened colour on her cheeks. But her mouth was twisted with unlovely scorn.

"All my life," she said, "I have been a pawn. I am used to it. It has no pain for me. Why should I go to France and make myself a laughing-stock? Maybe it would have been better if Richard had had me poisoned years ago."

"My lady—!"

"No, don't stop me, Robin of Wakefield. By the Mass, you might think a royal princess a fine bargain in the marriage-market, eh? Not so! Especially not when she is barren."

It was his turn to colour faintly and look down.

"That's not my business."

"Certainly it is not! But it is Wynford's! I tell you I should be grateful to him for sparing me. I am not."

"I know." Now he was facing her again, his voice quiet. "And that is a vile thing for a woman as fair as you to say."

At last. There was the note of gentleness allied to one of desire. Surely it was so. Yet she was beaten; she could not summon up any more anger to her defence. What good was it? He had injured her more now by his early apparent indifference than he had infuriated her by his pursuit.

"So you see me as fair?"

Like her husband, she was clearly at the challenging now. Robin was unsure. Should he answer like the smitten fool he was, after all? Or simply pick up the glove? He chose the latter course for safety's sake: she had not yet agreed to any plan to go to France.

"No man could see you as otherwise, madam. No man."

"Why did you turn from York to Lancaster?" she demanded forthrightly then.

She probably wanted him to hint that it had been for her.

"A grudge against King Edward," he said. "He took my woman."

"Your woman!" Margaret paled. Robin could have leapt forward and thrown his arms around her for the shatteringly welcome reaction. All pretence had left her under the shock. "I did not know," she stammered. She seemed defenceless; he pitied her so much it hurt.

"I care for her no more," he was able to say truthfully.

"No," very low. "I daresay you would not."

From below came the high screech of a peacock. She turned to look back over the stone balustrade again and this time Robin came slowly to her side. Unaccountably she was pointing down at the proud birds strutting beneath them on the grass. The Earl had long since retreated and the butts had been removed.

"Look," said Margaret, "how the peacocks have shed their tails and seem shorn of all their splendour. All my life I have felt like that. I told you I was accustomed to it, but that does not mean I care for it. I am a King's daughter, and I would like men to know it."

Her voice was quivering with injured pride.

"Then consent to go to France," urged Robin. "It is your only hope."

She was sighing, still deeply reluctant, though his words were cutting home.

"You must not tarry," he warned then. "Warwick's plans go forward—with or without you."

"I have heard it said a friend turned into an enemy is bitter and ruthless," she murmured. "I think I pity King Edward."

Suddenly, astonishingly, she had laid her beautiful hand briefly on his arm. He trembled like a fool.

"If I agree," she said, "what hope do you have of me?"

"Please be direct."

"I think you love me," she said with a quick, shattering frankness. "Can I trust myself with you? And my husband —is he just a little blind? Or desperate? There now, am I direct enough to please you?"

"You could be more so."

It was all he could do to keep his hands off her person. He breathed hard and, I cannot keep from her, he thought. Not much longer. I don't care what happens.

"Go now," said the Countess quietly. "I will travel to France with you, Robin of Wakefield. But for more you must understand you have to wait."

He went away. Confused on the one hand, elated beyond measure on the other. Surely she had made him a lover's promise, even after all her anger and ice? He had breached the resistance at last. His reward could not possibly be a disappointment.

EIGHT

Explosion came to Edward as the first winter weather came swirling in cold gusts over London, scattering dead brown leaves and sending shivers down the back.

It really was a thousand pities that Richard of Gloucester must choose to come bursting in on the King when he was still sharing a warm bed with Blanche la Belle. Gloucester's face looked black with fury.

"That treacherous bastard of a brother!" he bawled at the King who was pulling himself up in foolishly blinking haste. "He's betrayed us again! Gone off to Warwick and both of them gone marching up to Lincolnshire! It's outright war, Edward. We should have known it would be!"

Blanche had given a small shriek of fright, snatching up the covers round her bare, gleaming shoulders.

Edward reacted unusually. For a moment he just sat there hanging his head as if the expected news had been too much for him. He smote a helpless hand across the mattress.

"God's eyes!" he groaned. "So soon?"

"You ought to have slain Clarence long ago!" raged Gloucester.

"Ay, ay, it is very well for you, Richard," the King grumbled. "I am not so eager to spill my own kindred's blood. You might think to be grateful for it yourself one day."

Gloucester said nothing. He watched his brother get out

of the bed and reach for a gown to cover his tall nakedness. Edward was finely made, and Gloucester completely his opposite with his thin and rangy body: he could never view the King without jealousy. Even the whore's eyes were on him again and he had not left her side but a second since; women never looked at Richard of Gloucester like that.

Would he be so sparing of Edward's life if he were put to the test? Deep inside Richard there was a darkness that told him it would not be so.

"What shall you do?" he demanded harshly.

"Do?" rapped Edward. He was awake now, the lazy eyes had become steely. "There is no question. We march. The Queen must be removed to the Tower for her own safety until our return."

Gloucester strode out; already the palace was bursting into a fever of activity behind Edward's door. As it was opened a sea of faces seemed to be beyond, trying to gape inside. Edward himself slammed the portal shut on them as Blanche threw herself out of bed and ran to him in a weeping panic.

"What's to become of me? What of me? You send the Queen to the Tower but I am to take my chance!"

"Cover yourself, woman!" shouted Edward. He hurled her fur-trimmed cloak at her, and she wrapped herself in it, still crying hysterically. "I have a revolt on my hands! I cannot have a care for every light-of-love in the city!"

"You have no more bitter a foe than have I, my lord King!" shrieked Blanche. "And he alive and well in Warwick's camp—only thirsting for the chance to slit my throat!"

"Don't be a fool!" raged Edward. "He is dead."

In his own mind he knew perfectly well that could not be true, although he too felt afraid of Robin of Wakefield, he still could not but be glad of it. Such a man ought not to have been wasted so young.

"My lord, ensure my safety!" Blanche entreated wildly. She was genuinely terrified and Edward's heart was always soft for women. He supposed he owed her something.

"I'll give you money," he said. "You had best go back into the city where you must have friends. Don't be afraid, Blanche. I shall be back."

"Lancaster!" she quivered.

"Ay," his face had darkened again. His senses persisted in telling him this was no passing phase. The Yorkist sun was going into eclipse, though he must pray it would not be long-lasting.

"We'll be on our way up to Lincolnshire by dawn tomorrow," Edward told Blanche firmly. "Now enough of your wailing, woman. I've yet to go and face that of the Queen."

* * *

The news had reached Wynford. The King's army had evacuated London; it was streaming its steady way east to battle with the Lincoln insurgents. Warwick had vanished long since from the city together with the Duke of Clarence; they had formed an alliance with Lord Montague, Warwick's brother.

This was the kind of talk that made every Lancastrian catch his breath with awed excitement. Made his eyes gleam. London, almost open to attack! The Queen placed in the Tower for safety: that alone showed how vulnerable

Edward still was, even after eight solid years of rule.

It brightened Jasper Tudor into the best mood he had managed for weeks. It was irresistible. When a man thought the fortunes of his house were beaten at last it cowed him like a dog. Give him a whiff of some new triumph, some new hope, and he straightened his back and made bold his step.

The Earl of Pembroke could not help thinking of that sad, pale ghost of a man in his Tower quarters. King Henry VI. Did he have any inkling at all that his weary incarceration might again turn to glory? That the crown might sit on his head once more? The trouble with Henry was that he did not care enough about it. He ought to have been a monk.

A great barrel of red wine had been broached in celebration in the upper quarters of the castle. Wynford echoed with sounds of merriment and music. If the Earl was feeling oddly alone with his Countess departed under the care of Robin of Wakefield, it was not particularly apparent. He sat in the midst of his household to jest and drink with the rest, his men-at-arms included. His jester scampered about with a great jingling of cap and bells and a fine assortment of coarse jokes about Yorkists at which everyone roared with laughter.

But surely Richard Wynford had his mind on Margaret and Robin? He was not a fool. Tudor was eyeing him keenly.

"I'm drinking a toast to the release of King Henry," he said. "And one for the success of the lady Margaret's mission."

Wynford grunted.

"How long will it be before battle is joined between Warwick and Edward? A week? Two? Have they made their escape to the coast, I wonder? Travel will become dangerous now."

"I don't fear," said Tudor. "Warwick has been bold, moving without French aid, but he is astute. With the Kingmaker on our side we shall succeed, I know it."

"What if Edward should win this battle?"

"He has lost his full power. Depend on it. He's made too many enemies in these last years. I tell you we have every hope. There is King Henry, there is Edward, the Prince of Wales to lead Lancaster. And," he lowered his voice, "the possibility might occur to you that there is someone else, if only Queen Margaret will acknowledge her. Your wife, my lord."

Wynford almost choked with astonishment.

"The Countess?" he gasped. "Come, you run on, my lord!"

"She is the King's daughter. Senior to Edward, in fact."

"Never!" said Wynford, looking as if the idea filled him with sudden and intense excitement. "There has been no Queen-regnant in England since Matilda. And she had no luck with Englishmen."

"I but put the thought to you," gently. "Were, God forbid, King Henry and Prince Edward to perish—we could still keep the lady Margaret safe."

Wynford had risen to his feet and he paced about restlessly.

"Don't speak of this again," he told Tudor.

Jasper shrugged and reached for more wine. He had more than enough patience to wait.

NINE

At Losecoat Field, the two opposing sides met in the first real battle since the slaughter at Hexham. But then the banners of the bear and ragged staff had been ranged alongside those of the sun in splendour, now these were the devices of the two main warring participants. But the clamour was the same: the screaming and the furious clash of weapons. Edward the King was always to be found in the thick of any fight for he was no coward; neither was Richard of Gloucester. Yet as they cut and thrust their way through the howling ranks of the Kingmaker's rebels, unleashed at last, neither man caught any sight of either Warwick or Clarence the turncoat.

"Where are they?" Edward kept yelling. "God's face where are they? Am I to have no chance for my vengeance? None at all?"

He could hardly see through the blood that streamed down into his eyes from a flesh wound in the forehead; his helmet itself was dented with the impact of a blow that would have killed him without its protection. His armour felt insufferably hot and heavy, there was no time now to think of it. He must fight, fight. The quiet days of safety in London were far behind him with his frightened Queen.

"A Lancaster!" he could hear far too many enemy voices crying. "A Lancaster!"

"A York!" yelled his brother Richard in fury. "Into hell

with Lancaster and King Henry too!"

Edward's men seemed to take heart. They rushed into the fray with renewed energy, knights mounted high on coursers, footsoldiers with their round steel hats and breastplates, armed with shields and broadswords. The screaming was redoubling; the blood flowed faster.

"Edward the King! Edward the King!"

"They're turning!" bawled Hastings into Edward's ear. "Running, God be thanked, my liege!"

Edward reined in. It was true, from his vantage point on a rise of ground he could see Hastings was right. Warwick's insurgents had broken their line, hesitated and then suddenly split completely apart; and now they were scattering.

The King's men were not bothering to pursue them, but throwing down their arms and cheering. Incredible, thought Edward. They are that self-confident. Alas, this was a great moment, but he could not for the life of him share their triumph.

"They'll be back," he said to the astonished Hastings when he asked the King why he did not smile. "We have made no captures; none that matter."

But Richard of Gloucester had dismounted from his wounded courser to go tramping forward over a pile of dead bodies. He came back towards his brother, black with filth, and with dried blood streaking his armour; behind him he dragged one of Warwick's men. He threw the footsoldier down in front of Edward and kicked him. The prisoner coughed up blood.

"You," said Gloucester, "scum! Speak up to my lord the King and tell him where the Earl of Warwick is fled! By God, he disappoints me. I never saw him turn tail from a battle before."

"Mercy, my lord!"

"Mercy! None!" Gloucester laughed harshly. "You must think to jest, fellow."

"Where are Warwick and my lord of Clarence?" shouted Edward then. "Come, if you know it, tell me, and I'll spare your life."

The man was struggling up to his knees.

"Sire—Sire—" he panted. "I know little! My lord of Warwick was never with us. It was said he was ready to cross to France with your brother before we ever came face to face with you."

Hastings observed the King's face paling to a deathly hue.

"Ay," said Edward hollowly. He understood now. All this was for Margaret of Anjou's benefit. She would not fail to take notice this time. He turned away, he had almost forgotten the wretched informant. Gloucester took the opportunity of the King's inattention and plunged his sword into the captive man's chest clean up to the hilt. His last scream echoed up horridly, dying into a whimper and a faint rattle in the throat. Richard withdrew the blade, grinning, wiping it on the grass.

"I gave my promise," said Edward to him angrily then.

"What did he matter?" countered Gloucester. "So perish all traitors."

"I have learned this," said the King wearily, "that there are far too many of them. Too many for us to kill them all."

* * *

Warwick was at Calais with Clarence. That was the obvious destination then, for Robin of Wakefield and the Countess of Wynford. They had left the castle in extreme secrecy, taking with them only the most scant escort of her husband's men, and even those had been scheduled to leave them at the coast.

Parting between the Wynfords' had been odd; strained. If Robin had not seen affection on Margaret's part there had certainly been a real reluctance to go at last from her husband's side. Reluctance which ought to have given warning that he was far more important to her sense of security than Margaret herself was aware of.

But nothing could be said. She would only have retorted, Robin knew, that it was none of his business, so cool did she appear to be towards him again. Unkindly, he thought with some resentment, unjustly. Deeply as he adored her beauty she was beginning to puzzle him, and sadden him.

Despite the disturbed state of the land after Losecoat, their journey across country was not perilous; they reached Dover in good time and found passage on a small fishing-boat. The captain peered with keen curiosity at the hooded, tall figure of the lady and demanded extra money for the quality. Irritated, Robin paid up, and with a surly grunt they were allowed aboard.

Margaret sought the evilly cramped and smelly quarters allotted to her at once. She sat down on a barrel of tar looking miserable, folding her cloak tightly about her as the small vessel cast off from the beach and headed out into the Channel. The wind was rising and so was the sea; and before long the fishing-boat was tossing and heaving its way over the waves, driven before the gale.

Her face had gone white. Wordlessly the stronger Robin poured out wine from a flask and forced it into her hand.

"Drink."

"I don't want it."

"Drink!" He found himself almost shouting at her above the noise of the outside elements. "Drink, lady, or I'll cuff you into unconsciousness of your miseries and that is a promise!"

What made him so angry with her? So ready—indeed almost desirous—of carrying out the threat he made? She looked up at him confounded, the hazel eyes clouded with sudden doubtful respect. By the Mass, he had actually done good by his tirade.

"You mean that, don't you?" she whispered. "Have I hurt you so much?"

"Lady," furiously, "there are times when I do not know what you have done to me. At least with Blanche la Belle I knew what the fault was; she was too fond of men and riches. But you—you don't seem to know what you want of anything or anybody for two days at a time."

Margaret drank the wine slowly. It did her good; some of the colour came back to her wan cheeks. She handed him back the empty cup.

"Please leave me alone now," she said.

"Gladly!" Robin snapped at her, turning to go.

She stopped him as he would have bent his head to go striding out of the low door.

"Robin! You ought not to think me ungrateful for your efforts."

"I read more than that into your promises and you know it." He spoke in a smothered tone, keeping his back to her. "You deceived me."

"I am confused," she protested. "You cannot imagine the emotions which torture me. Should I have left Wynford? Should I lower myself if for the last time, to my termagant mother? Is it worth it for any of us?"

"That is not what you said before, my lady."

"You must try to understand."

"I understand that you gave me hope of yourself and have now retracted."

"No," gently. "Not retracted. I could not do that. I have some affection for my husband and I was shaken to part with him as I had not expected to be. Knowing that I would turn in love to you—that it was inevitable."

He turned to stare at her. In the dim and reeking box of a cabin, she only seemed the lovelier, the more desirable. She had thrown back her hood and much of the fine copper hair hung round her shoulders, curling.

"I don't come back again, lady," he said forcefully, "unless you give me your word never to push me away for caprice. If you do not love me—that is different."

"Robin," softly. She held out both her hands to him. In a trice he had gone to her and seized them passionately. She wept a little, and her head rested on his broad shoulder gratefully. He wound his arms tightly around her shaking body.

"Don't be afraid," he tried to soothe her. "I don't want to lower your pride. I'll walk gladly in your shadow if that's what I must do. The Queen will acknowledge you: I know it. I'll serve you as you choose and not expect more."

"But you will!" she pulled back, looking earnestly at him. She stroked his face lightly with one hand. "You would not be a proud man if it was not so! It is too late perhaps for me to draw back—but not for you."

He understood that well enough. She would love him yet make, in the end, a pretty fool out of him. She was Wynford's wife and nothing would make her change that. She would be his mistress, never any more. And he would always have to wait tamely for her. That, said his own pride and common sense sternly, was unacceptable. Unmanly. It was worse than taking Blanche back after Edward had been using her.

But Robin said nothing. Only tightened his arms around the Countess of Wynford's beautiful form and rested his cheek with pleasure against the shining waft of her perfumed hair. She moved her head again and with a certain, almost innocent dignity, she lifted her face towards him so that he could cover it with shatteringly violent kisses which did not seem to terrify her at all. For possession itself would come later, at some other place which she would name, not now.

* * *

Warwick was seated with his family in the old great hall of the castle at Calais which was his to command. If the English hold on France had again become tenuous in this last twenty years, Calais still remained solidly in their hands. Of course the days of Agincourt glory were long since done: the Maid of Orleans long since burnt to ashes for her part in freeing her people, and her Dauphin, from the domination of the King; then Henry V. The present, sad, mad Henry VI had fulfilled all too well the old prophecy "Henry born at Monmouth shall gain all: Henry born at Windsor shall lose all." Henry V had forbidden Catherine the Fair to bear his son at Windsor, but she had disobeyed him. Who knew just how many ills had sprouted out of that wifely transgression?

But these thoughts were not for Warwick now. Everything looked well for him, not even the defeat of his troops at Losecoat Field had thrown him from his current perch of confidence. Edward would be driven out of England soon and Warwick would be ready to go leaping back, to seize London and let King Henry out of his cell to parade like a puppet for him again.

And Margaret of Anjou? Louis XI was still working on her; her own father René King of Sicily, was anxiously trying to persuade his younger daughter to listen to my lord of Warwick's overtures. Up to now the Queen was still sulking in Verdun, simmering over her wrongs. But messengers rode back and forth to her castle; she was given little peace. Moreover her son, Edward, was said to be growing restless, for he was of an age to want to be about fighting for his rights—and he had set eyes on the Kingmaker's other daughter, Anne Neville.

Margaret of Anjou would move. She must. Louis would begin to threaten her with exile from France as well if she did not show some real sign of being willing to accept the noble aid so lavishly being offered her, solely out of spite.

Such was Warwick's feeling that success was to come, that he was not in the least shaken to be told of the new arrivals at the castle.

"My lord of Wakefield?"

Clarence, of course looked up, shaken. He half rose from his chair; his Duchess admonished him to sit again. Anne Neville tended to giggle.

"But surely—?" he began.

"I have many secrets," smiled Warwick thinly. "My lord's desertion to my cause—our cause, my lord Duke; was but one of them. Yes, you are right, it is the same lord whom Hastings had sent men to kill. Do you blame him for coming to me?"

How could Clarence do that, with his history of defections? But he could not stop the glower of outrage as Robin came into the hall. Though it changed with comic rapidity as he observed his companion.

"God's body," said Clarence, muffled with shock. It had never been his privilege to see the lady Margaret before, like others, he knew nothing of her existence. But he did know the look of Margaret of Anjou and King Henry VI. And of Edward, Prince of Wales.

Warwick had risen at once, looking suddenly grave. The way he went to Margaret and bent the knee before her was more than enough to confirm the stammering Clarence's conviction.

"My lady Margaret," Warwick was murmuring. "I had not dared to hope."

So he had done it; Wakefield's boast had been no idle one after all. How right Warwick had been to take the chance with this man! This was the final seal on his run of triumph: it must be. Confront the Queen with her rejected daughter and she would crumble; not even her iron will would stand up against the shock and so many united pleas.

Margaret smiled remotely, giving Warwick her hand to kiss.

"I have come a long way," she said, "in a foul fishing-smack, to seek for your rights, my lord. But mostly for my own."

"It is understood, gracious lady. Understood. God willing I shall bring your mother out of her eyrie at Kuerere before the month is ended. And then—!"

"Ah, and then?" she murmured slightly cynically. "England for Lancaster again? If Edward will allow it."

"My lady, you dishonour your own inheritance by that!

Have I not entreated you before to trust my word?"

Margaret was staring beyond Warwick, towards his two lovely daughters and George of Clarence. Her skin prickled as though she still felt herself very much in the presence of enemies. She thought she read her absent mother's distrusts and hatreds with complete cognisance: it must be desperately hard to accept the Kingmaker as a new ally.

"I do not want the Queen to know I am here yet," she said firmly.

Nothing could prejudice her cause more at this juncture than for her mother to think she was Warwick's henchwoman before Margaret of Anjou had been forced into her own acknowledgement. She supposed Warwick guessed her purpose by his scornful, short laugh, but there was little doubt he recognised wisdom in the proposal too.

"I shall see to it that she does not," he replied. "We shall play a better game than that, my lady. And both win what we want."

He took her hand and led her out of the hall as though he urgently needed private words with her. Alert, Robin of Wakefield followed.

Clarence was on his feet again, pacing with intense agitation below the tall windows, hands clasped tightly behind his back. He scowled, he looked almost feverish. Anne Neville had made her own excuses and departed, sensing that her sister and brother-in-law wanted to be alone in their turn.

"What's amiss with you, my lord?" demanded Duchess Isabel.

"I cannot help myself!" Clarence said to her. "I feel as though my head spins. News such as this! Knowledge such as this! The Queen had a daughter long before she had

Prince Edward—by the Mass, if I could but tell the King! To see his face!"

"My lord, it will suit you best to remember your brother is not called the King at Calais!"

"No," muttered Clarence, "no. But I thought there was only mad Henry and the Prince of Wales."

He must mean those were the ones he had thought of as standing in his way to the throne. Isabel, who had known of Margaret's existence for some time, hesitated. Was she really some kind of danger to her own ambitious plans? But she dismissed the idea.

"Don't fear," she told Clarence. "Have you not realised? Why do you think her existence was denied, my lord? She was said to have her father's curse."

Clarence stopped.

"Insanity?" he croaked.

"Ay, just so. Watch her well and I think you will perceive it in time."

"She looked sane enough to me."

"So did King Henry on his good days. All know he is harmless enough, withal, but he is still mad."

Clarence said no more. He reseated himself, still scowling, still restless. Alas, this family bond that tied him to York persisted in telling him he ought to run fast to Edward and tell him about Margaret Wynford. For, whether the woman was stricken as his wife suggested, or not, she existed. And that was the point.

* * *

Despite himself, Robin of Wakefield was becoming a very uneasy man. The Countess tortured him with her seemingly endless staving off of their becoming real lovers—and yet the day had appeared so close aboard that wretched fishing vessel. But no: almost as soon as he had brought her safe to Calais, a new veil had descended between them. Margaret kept a lonely vigil often in her own quarters, brooding no doubt on her mother's likely greeting of her. Or, damn her, was she somehow pining for Wynford? Robin could not know. He could only feel bitter and wounded by turn. So much so, that when he finally received the summons to go to her he could have torn it across and burnt it in the flickering candle-flames lighting his quarters.

Outside the wind had risen and it was soughing in a strange and dispirited way about the towers of the castle. It filled his mind with chill foreboding. Yet for all that, he knew he must go to her. Whatever this bond was between them it must be forged fast, even though it bid fair to destroy them both.

How sad he often caught her looking, the pain in her eyes hardly concealed. And was there not that same pain in the words of this letter? 'I am cold, Robin. Too much alone'.

He had been a fool to love her and a fool to enmesh himself in her business but the deed was done. Robin blew out his candle and made his way softly towards her part of the castle. She had been given lodgings near to the Warwicks and the Clarences, as befitted her rank. Several guards sleepily watched him go by, leaning on their pikes. Those outside the Countess' door obviously had their instructions, for they stood aside for him without query. The girl Warwick had allotted to serve Margaret let Robin in with a smile and a curtsey.

He stood silently waiting in this very comfortable place and stared about him warily. No sign of the Countess?

The maid was smiling again now and bringing him wine.

"The lady said to drink, sir, and then to go to her. Beyond the curtain."

She waved a hand towards the hanging in question, deep red velvet no doubt to keep the draught out of the bedchamber. The Countess was not bothering to be too discreet with the servants. Surely that was unwise. Robin felt yet more ill at ease, but the girl had already gone out of the door and left him to be assailed by a silence even deeper than that in his own quarters. Except for the wind, of course; its mournful sigh seemed determined to follow him.

Robin shook himself, drained his cup dry and went striding finally across to the mysterious curtain; he lifted it and stood there, staring in on the Countess. He was speechless. She was sitting still as a statue in the middle of the big bed, illuminated by the several candles placed in the wall-holder, copper hair spilling down in profusion, unencumbered by any binding. There was no smile on her madonna-like face but as he looked at her she raised both arms towards him and the covers over her naked body fell away. She gleamed like pure white marble. He could believe for a moment that she would be just as cold to touch.

But:

"You see?" she asked him, very low. "Once I have made up my mind I do not hold back. I shall not prove a disappointment to you, Robin. It is true I have known no man but my husband but he has never found me to be frigid. I love you. I do love you, my lord. Inasmuch as a woman like myself can love."

"What do you mean?" asked Robin hoarsely. "Either

you love me or you don't."

"Warwick has hope of the Queen coming from Verdun before Christmastide," she said almost dreamily.

"Ah, I see. I am not good enough. Not for a Princess. Hardly for a Countess!"

"Forgive me—" she sounded a little wretched now—"but I am no liar. Go away, Robin, if I do not suit you as I am."

"Go away?" He was advancing towards the bed, his hands already at the fastenings of his doublet. "You mock me. You need me."

"I do," she sighed. "And I will wrong you."

She moved over and waited for him, her eyes flickering with interest over his well-muscled body and narrow hips. She did not seem in the least embarrassed.

Robin lifted the covers and slid into bed beside her, turning her unresisting form towards him at once. She saw him close his eyes with the sheer pleasure of knowing her flesh encompassed by his; of knowing he could do his will with her. Then real desire awoke. His hands dug hard into the softness of her breasts and he was almost stifling her with more of his furious kissing. He progressed to love her, and she was aroused quickly to the burning kind of response she had not really known before; her body blended with his and she locked fierce fingers into the back of his neck, digging in her nails. At last they fell apart, shaking, panting for breath. Robin moved to the side of her, shoulders heaving, striving to recover himself.

Margaret lay quietly now, once her own breathing had slowed. She put out one hand to stroke his bare arm gently. He raised himself up to stare down at her with oddly sunken eyes and this time she laughed softly.

"Now what of your Blanche la Belle?" she went so far

as to tease.

The truth was that he found them comparable but it would be manifestly discourteous to say that. Besides the Countess had a certain mysterious depth of fascination that did not lift simply because he had made use of her beautiful body.

"I see only you," said Robin truthfully. "Only you."

Margaret nodded; that satisfied her. She turned her head to one side and closed her eyes.

TEN

It did not, of course, take long for the news to circulate. The Countess of Wynford had taken a lover by no means of her own station. Neither was any real effort made by either party to conceal the fact. Apart from being separated at table, they were seen almost everywhere together. Walking, laughing, on the battlements, and strolling in the gardens. Riding out into the town where curious-eyed foreigners gathered eagerly to watch them and marvel at the woman's fairness. Sometimes the Warwicks joined them on hunting-parties; often they were to be seen dancing together in the great hall of Calais—apparently without any reluctance on the Earl's part. Maybe his womenfolk demurred. Maybe they had even begun to dislike Margaret a little for her remoteness with them; indeed she seemed not to care much for feminine company. Perhaps that was because she had been so early deprived of it.

"This is not right," grumbled the Countess of Warwick to her husband. "Not meet for our daughter Anne to witness. Isabel is different: she is married and has seen much of the world."

"Pish," said Warwick contemptuously, "I'll have other interests for the lady soon."

"What if this talk drifts back to England? To Wynford? Do you expect him to remain your friend—allowing his wife to be seduced under your nose?"

"I fancy my lord Earl knows better than that," wryly. "The lady Margaret calls the tune of her fancy and ever did so from what I hear."

"You said they were well-matched!"

"They are. Is it so terrible that she should find a little enjoyment on the side, my love? Are you telling me Wynford is faithful to her?"

Warwick did not bother to answer. He was waving newly arrived parchment at her instead.

"Read this," he said. "From his Most Christian Majesty, Louis XI. We have succeeded, wife, at last. The King has finally persuaded Queen Margaret to agree to a meeting at Tours."

"Tours!" The Countess flushed with enthusiasm at once, spitefulness forgotten. "Richard, dare we hope to unbend that woman's spirit? Dare we?"

"We have allies," said Warwick with meaning. "Prince Edward has long cherished Anne. The French want Queen Margaret off their hands if possible. And then there is her daughter."

"Ay," she said. "The Princess Margaret! Now she may make or break us."

"I do not fear," said Warwick with conviction. "And carp how you will, wife, I think it is thanks to the company of Robin of Wakefield that my lady no longer fears either. She will prevail upon her mother this time. I feel it in my bones."

* * *

Winter had awarded France a bright, sunny day in the midst of December. It was cold, but everywhere the sunshine renewed old faded hues; lent a sheen to sloping rooftops, and glanced through bare-branched trees in glistening patterns. For the jingling cavalcade coming down the rutted road towards the splendid and ancient city of Tours, an accompanying lift of the spirit was inevitable. Not even the sourest face of Queen Margaret could defy it, though few women could wear a sourer one if they chose.

She rode at the head of her party, a tall and splendid woman, whose royal dignity could never be doubted. Although her face was now haughty and hawklike, much sunken due to the perilous course of her enormous troubles, she had once been one of the greatest beauties of Europe. Her rich golden hair was turned to grey now, her soft skin pitted by old disease, but her bearing and air of massive authority still made it very plain she was a Queen.

Tours had come into sight with its strong walls and its myriad of towers. Royal banners flew over the castle; that of the King of France principally, but also the banner of King René of Sicily, Margaret of Anjou's father. She felt warmed by the thought that so many friends must be gathered there to greet her from her lonely seclusion in Verdun. But not so pleased to remember the object of the journey: to meet with my lord, the viper Earl of Warwick.

The Queen had expected to be received honourably, but she was startled to find that she was to be met outside the city.

"See, gracious lady mother!" cried out the handsome Prince Edward from where he rode at her side. "It is Louis himself!"

And the King of Sicily, and the Count and Countess de Vaudemont. Margaret of Anjou felt herself flush with pleasure, with excitement. She had great affection for her family, for her father and stepmother; for her sister and brother-in-law. She hardly had any eyes for the cool Louis XI at all, even though it was to the King of France she must turn in courtesy at once as her pages assisted her from the back of her courser. He greeted her in a fashion almost too friendly for comfort, considering she knew what plan lurked at the back of all this.

"Welcome," said Louis, "right noble Queen."

"We have drawn you forth at last, madame," murmured Count Ferry de Vaudemonte kindly, watching as the Queen shared the embraces first of her father and his second wife, Jeanne de Laval. She turned then to her sister, Yolante, and both women were weeping a little.

"Ay," said the Queen finally, drawing back and dabbing at her eyes, "and much affected I am by it. My son"—she was holding out a hand to Prince Edward to bring him forward—"it is for me to try to see that these good people have gathered here to help mend our fortunes this day."

That was brave talk and the King of France guessed it. He was exchanging a glance with King René, and both of them were wondering the same thing. Should the mercurial Queen Margaret be presented with Warwick first, or with her repudiated daughter? Would she, despite her emotional state, end again by rejecting them both?

The party mounted up for the second time and now it formed a procession winding its way into the city of Tours. Splashed with the brilliant colours of the cloaks and gowns; glistening with the play of sunlight on the bright armour. Trumpets were shrilling and banners waving; a large detachment of footsoldiers marched on ahead as escort, keeping in time to the beat of the kettledrums.

* * *

The Countess of Wynford saw them coming from her viewpoint in the castle. She had turned deathly pale and both hands were suddenly clenched together beneath her heart.

"Holy God," she whispered. "I think I cannot do it after all. I think I cannot face her."

It was Anne Neville, kind-hearted and pretty, who put an arm about her shoulders. The Countess of Warwick and the Duchess of Clarence held back, uncertain.

"Lady," said Anne persuasively, "you know you have come too far to go back. Your mother has wronged you and in her heart she knows that. You must at least give her the chance to make amends."

"You cannot know how it feels," protested the Countess.

"No, lady, I cannot. But I know your courage is more than equal to the task."

Margaret looked at her. It was quite impossible to dislike Anne; her gentleness and concern for others was genuine. She was astonishingly different from the rest of her cold and ambitious kindred.

"You," said Margaret finally, "would make a magnificent bride for my brother."

At that the youngest Warwick girl flushed, then smiled as if with gratitude.

"And you are the first Lancastrian to say so, madame. I thank you. May your words bring both of us good luck.

Robin of Wakefield had come into the chamber with a slightly uncomfortable air about him. Margaret thought he looked surpassingly handsome in his armour, yet he was always the tough soldier. Not for the first time it passed through her mind, however, that he might still feel it strange to be wearing Warwick's colours. How flattered did she feel that this man had chosen to follow her way as he had? Very flattered, she supposed. Alas, she wished she had not ceased to feel the eager, heart-stopping urge for his company that she had been tormented with at Wynford. She still felt desire for him, but she was no longer sure that she knew genuine affection. It was since his possession of her, of course. Lust remained but she had begun to lie now when she said she loved him. It was not the same with him, and he did not seem to have noticed any alteration in her.

She managed to summon up a brilliant smile for his benefit, and with only a cursory bow to the other women who started to glare at once, he addressed himself to her.

"My lady, His Grace the King of France requires you to present yourself in the hall."

"To whom?" Margaret's voice trembled over the formalities.

"To Her Grace, the Queen of England."

Margaret swallowed hard, grateful for the quick touch of Anne's hand on her sleeve.

"Go now," the girl whispered. "Go"

The Duchess was moving forward as if in a dream, placing one heavily ringed hand on Robin's armour-plated arm. He led her carefully out and slowly down the stone steps, her long train slithering softly down behind them. She looked like a queen herself in all that gold damask, thickly embroidered with sparkling jewels and thread. A light silver gauze floated from the tip of her gold head-dress: a tremendous necklace of gold and rubies lay on her neck.

He brought her to a sudden halt; she stared at him.

"One thing only," he said quietly, "before you go on, my lady. Take this from me."

He was holding out the package he had bought for Blanche. He ought to have given it to Margaret before, not made the foolish mistake of keeping it. Why, when the girl certainly meant nothing to him any more?

Margaret had taken it wordlessly and removed the tattered wrapping. The ring winked its green fire up at her. A strange, jealous colour—green.

"This is a wedding-ring," she said oddly.

"Wear it, lady. To please me."

She sighed. She did not understand him, confusing her further at a moment like this. But probably he meant it as a good luck charm, given much in the spirit with which Anne Neville had spoken. She took it and slid it on to the index finger of her left hand, but amongst the splendour of so many other rings it seemed lost. His face shadowed.

He had indeed intended the gift as an omen. For him at least, it now appeared to be a bad one.

"We must hurry on," she was saying nervously, her eyes fixed on the door to the hall behind which destiny waited.

"Come then," said Robin heavily.

She would go in there as a Countess and come out an acknowledged Princess: he knew it.

What then? Any man would be a fool to have faith in romantic fancies such as being able to wed with royalty—ay, even if the husband who stood in the way was to be somehow removed. He had permitted himself to indulge in them though. More idiot he.

* * *

Warwick, still keeping out of the way, had everything arranged. As the Countess approached, he gave the signal for a short fanfare.

The hall was crowded with people and in the midst of them the two Kings, with Queen Margaret and Queen Charlotte of Savoy, Louis XI's wife who was great with child, and Queen Jeanne Laval. Distinguished company indeed. Anyone might be forgiven for finding a falter in their step as they entered such an arena, and it was for this that Warwick had provided. He had guessed a psychological advantage would be scored at once by bringing in the glittering stranger to the accompaniment of trumpets. It would shake all these proud royals into realising immediately that this was a woman of no ordinary quality. Moreover, it was bound to have a similar effect on the Countess.

Warwick was hiding behind the heavy curtains, watching, holding his breath. He had wanted to see the hall plunged into astonished, blinking silence as Margaret appeared. He was not disappointed. Not in the company and after the first trauma, not in her.

Into that marvelling place she came, head held high, walking with grace and pride that fair outdid all of them. Her clear eyes were fixed on the Queen of England—a face which, confronted with her, turned a deathly white where it had been glowing with colour a moment before. Margaret of Anjou's weary eyes seemed to sink even further into her head, she was seen to sway on her feet and Prince Edward threw out a swift and sustaining hand to her. The young man gazed confounded at the Countess in his turn. There was really no need to say anything; the family resemblance was too great.

Margaret went forward. No one impeded her progress; the path to her mother was clear. She went up to the shrinking woman, regarded her with a brief steadiness and then sank to her knees in front of her, head bent.

"Your Grace," she said in a quivering voice, "lady and mother. You know well how many years have passed during which I have begged of you for my rights. By messages and by gifts. None have you heeded. I protest before this company of your unkindness and present my own person on this occasion. That has been made possible by the persuasions of one to whom you ought to be grateful. Madame" —she looked up now and suddenly her countenance was a pleading, almost passionate one—"I ask you in honesty, what is there in me that you should reject me so? I am the true daughter of King Henry and yourself; the lord Edward is my true brother! You break my heart, beloved lady, to spurn me. Why do you continue ashamed of me?"

The Queen was trembling violently. She seemed unable to speak, as though her tongue had swollen in her mouth.

"Madame!" Prince Edward cried instead. "What have you done? Is this the sister you told me had died in her cradle? Is this fairest of women really of my blood? By God," fiercely, "of course she is! How could she be anyone else?"

Edward completely overstepped royal etiquette. He was shocked and angry, angry to think his adored mother had made a fool out of him. He went to Margaret and with his own strong young hands he raised her up, put his arms around her and kissed her on the cheek. He tasted tears; he whispered "Courage!" into her ears and turned back to his whey-faced, still horrified mother.

"Madame, you must say something!" demanded Edward.

The Queen worshipped him. His scorn wounded her as no other's was capable of doing. Her head was spinning; she felt physically sick with shock. What wonder when this incredible ghost of a woman whose existence she had tried to forget for the easing of her own conscience, was suddenly conjured up before her?

When she could indeed see for herself the quality of the first child born of her, a child she had expected to run mad and to die before she was ten years of age. It appeared most profoundly not so. And in her treatment of this beautiful daughter since she had married her off to Wynford to keep her out of the way, she had most certainly sinned. Deeply.

But no one wanted to feel such a smart of guilt. She had known excuses enough since the wars had begun to forget about her namesake, immured in the foothills of Wales.

"This," she almost hissed at both Margaret and Edward at last, "is ill done!"

"Madame!" protested the Prince.

"It is ill done, I say! And by Warwick! Is that not so? Is that not the one to whom I am supposed to languish in gratitude?"

What directed her into it Margaret never knew. Perhaps she understood her fiery mother with one half of her own diversive personality: that half Warwick had been unable to direct or control. She saw only the Queen of England still determined on her iron-hard stand as before, despite her appearance. That her last, desperate venture would fail again if only for the sake of the Queen's incredible stubbornness, her violent reluctance to admit herself in the wrong. Force like that was only respectful of force. Away with the tears and the supplication.

Margaret, trembling herself, but this time with wrath, confronted her mother. Her face was hardly six inches away from the Queen's, her hands fierce on her thin arms, clutching at her.

"I will hear no more of this!" she shouted at her. "By the Mass, Your Grace, what good fortune do you ever expect for my brother—my father—the house of Lancaster! Did you ever think that your vile treatment of me since my birth had singled you out to be cursed? To let York grind Lancaster into the dust? If you have not thought of it, then begin to do so now! Before it is finally too late!"

A universal gasp had filled the hall. The horrified silence brought Warwick out in stunned admiration from his hiding-place. For the astuteness of the Earl told him, as it did not tell the rest, that the Duchess must have struck a master-blow. He could never have hoped for her to be so clever. Desperate, yes. And see what his boldness had brought him now.

The proud harridan of a Queen was shrinking from her enraged daughter's grasp. She looked hunted, beaten. Warwick had never imagined such a thing.

"Leave hold of me, girl!" Margaret of Anjou was croaking. "Leave hold!"

"No, I shall not! Not until you give me back my rights, and my title of Princess of England! Restore me to that honour you have denied me since my birth, and for which my husband has had to suffer in his turn! What right had you to ask such an existence of either of us, madame? Call me daughter! I demand it. Call me daughter!"

The Queen was reeling, grasping desperately at Prince Edward's arm.

"By the Face!" she choked. "After all the warmth of your ire is enough to convince me you are as accursed as I always believed you! You may deceive others, but not me!"

"What do you mean?" shrieked Margaret. "What lies

would you have this company believe?"

"You spoke of honour," said Margaret of Anjou hoarsely, "then in honour take your hands from me. When, in God's name, may any child handle her parent so?"

What had she said? What had this magnificent woman drawn from her, despite the full force of her own resistance? Was it still possible the Queen had been wrong, that her first-born had been whole in mind as well as body? She simply could not acknowledge that. But she had most certainly acknowledged that this was her child. It was too late to regress.

Margaret herself was holding her breath, feeling dizzy, overwhelmed. She had won. The victory was hard to contemplate.

"Madame," she whispered at last, "I pray you, tell your mind loudly to all these folk."

Still leaning on the Prince's arm, the Queen was evidently struggling against her own instincts. But somehow she was nodding, and raising her voice.

"Margaret Wynford, I proclaim you my true daughter and the daughter of King Henry VI. My lords and ladies—" she stared around her almost desperately—"this is the Princess Margaret of England. In future all rightful homage and loyalty shall be paid to her by those who follow the house of Lancaster. There," she glared at Margaret, "it is said."

There would be no opportunity for a warmly, shatteringly grateful reply. The words froze on Margaret's lips as the Queen pushed Prince Edward away and began to walk, stiff as a ramrod, out of the hall.

It was understandable that she should feel overcome with emotion—and obvious that she was the prey to the bitterest chagrin and thought herself tricked. She must make her escape to seek for sanity and calm again.

* * *

It was not a good moment to come face to face with Warwick. She recoiled from him indeed, as though he had been some poisonous serpent.

"No!" Queen Margaret hurled at him. "No! Not you!"

"By your leave, Your Grace, for King Henry's sake you should not speak so to me."

Warwick's voice was curt. In this moment it was quite impossible for either side to forget the vicious past. Yet both of them must. He must remember that.

"I will not have you in my party!" cried the Queen. "I cannot pardon you, Warwick! You waste your time with your games! I have listened to all manner of persuasions else I would not be here. But the moment I see your face, I know I waste my time!"

The King of France was striding over.

"Lady," he addressed the Queen icily, "this is my country and I do not care to hear you speak to the Earl so. You know he is ready to help you; he has taken oath on that before me!"

"But not before me!"

"As God is my judge, Your Grace," said Warwick forcefully, "I am ready to do that even now!"

"For sure," she murmured bitterly, "God will be your judge one day. You will burn in hell for your perfidy. I hate you, Warwick. It is useless to try to change that."

"Then accept my lord's help without such an attempt," said Louis smoothly. "I ought to remind Your Grace that you came to France with mighty plans to return to your own land with an army at your back. I guarantee you that. If I see that there is some hope of success, and that my men will not be wasted. Take my lord Earl as your general and you will give me confidence."

The Queen was glaring at Warwick. Tears of frustration were threatening to begin. She fought hard to keep them concealed from him. This, when she was still stunned from confrontation with her daughter, was too much. Everyone was against her, even Prince Edward. She could see that the dainty Anne Neville had gone to him in the distance, that he was smiling and taking her hand.

That was almost as ill a sight as perfidious Clarence, King Edward's traitor brother, a welcome guest in Warwick's hall as well. Tours! They had lured her here to make a joint sacrifice of her, the Countess of Wynford included. She would not forget.

"I can give no answer now," the Queen said low and angrily. "Your pardon, brother of France. I can give no answer now!"

She kicked her long train out at the back and swept away.

ELEVEN

The battle of words and recriminations had begun; it was to last long. For Queen Margaret, to Warwick, still persisted in being the most obdurate of women. The harder she was pressurised from outside, even by her friends, to yield; the more she strove to cling to her own ideals. Yet she knew she was bound in the end to lose. Friendship persisted in springing up between the Nevilles and her own partisans; Prince Edward made no secret of his courtship of the lady Anne. When the Earl of Oxford came to make peace with Margaret of Anjou at Angers, he brought news of an England in real rebellion against York. The Queen could not resist excitement.

"Your Grace," Oxford urged her, "strike now. Delay is dangerous. Accept Warwick's offers, I beg you. We all beg you."

The Queen sighed. She felt beaten. And Warwick, who hung about her places of residence ever-watchful and waiting, must know that she was.

"You are against me," she said miserably, "the pack of you! And she, that girl of mine that Warwick hauled here from England—she is as bad as the rest! He brought her here to bedevil my mind; weaken me! He has succeeded and to be honest with you I curse them both."

That was true enough, thought Prince Edward sadly, thinking of the very silent departure of the Countess Margaret to Amboise in the train of the French Queen, scarce two days after her mother had publicly acknowledged her. The decision that Margaret should go to Amboise was illustrative of the Queen's real attitude towards her: she did not want her in her company if it could possibly be avoided.

Edward felt sorry for his beautiful sister. He had already begun to know some affection for her, puzzling enigma though she still seemed to him—who had thought her dead at birth.

"Madame," he said to the Queen, "you are unkind to the lady Margaret. She wishes only for your approbation."

The Queen's lip curled.

"She is unlikely to find it. Let her be content with what she has. A place at Queen Charlotte's side; her rank and privileges. That is enough for anyone. By the Mass, she has almost more than me."

"A crown still awaits you at Westminster," retorted the Prince, "if only you will give Warwick the word."

* * *

Margaret Wynford was lonely. Dejected. In that astonishing moment of triumph over her mother, that had not seemed possible. She had expected to remain on the crest of the wave after so many years of disappointment, yet it was only short hours after she had despatched the joyful tidings back to Richard Wynford, that black, soul-numbing depressions began a steady daily attack on her everyday living. Despite her enviable position at Amboise, they continued to come, and to grow stronger. The early pleasures of finding herself amidst such luxury, the object of marvelling French courtiers' interest soon wore thin. The dark days of winter were not helping her. The shadows had come down on her glowingly lovely countenance and she knew people were beginning to whisper and to wonder what could be amiss. Was it simply that the handsome Robin of Wakefield was still at Calais?

No, said the better-informed. The Countess sees that her mother hates her and that wounds her deep. More fool her, to trouble so about a termagant like Queen Margaret.

And so, for Margaret Wynford, weary days. Endless days, waiting patiently with a gaggle of other high-born women for Queen Charlotte to begin her lying-in. Men were not permitted anywhere near their vicinity at a time like this. Men! Who was she really longing for? Margaret sometimes asked herself. Wynford's quiet strength, which she had come to miss very much? Or Robin's ardour? Probably the truth was that she missed them both and felt horridly unable to stand fast on her own.

She wrestled valiantly with the growing darknesses in her mind, conscious that they strove to smother everything that hurt her and leave her a wan thing without any real character of her own, a personality fit only to be a puppet. With crashing terror, she realised what this was: it was the disease that crippled her father, King Henry.

Her mother knew. Bitter, scathing Queen Margaret knew. Saw all too clearly through the image her daughter presented to her; knew she was as accursed as she had always believed.

"No!" Margaret wept to herself with passion. "No! I will not allow it! Robin, where are you? If only there was but a moment of comfort!"

* * *

Perhaps it was drawing near. Queen Charlotte had taken to her bedchamber at last, the hangings were drawn tight across the narrow windows, and the chambers were heavy with the purifying fumes burning in small dishes. In her curtained bed, Queen Charlotte lay groaning. Margaret found herself watching with jealousy; she knew she had clenched her hand tightly around Robin's ring. All her adult life she had tried to persuade herself that it was Richard Wynford's fault she had borne no children. But it was not so. She was not even pregnant by Robin, grateful though she would have been for it, despite the scandal. It would have relieved her from the stigma of being barren. And this foolish woman lay in her bed and wept, then screamed. Margaret thought she would have been glad to endure her torments for the triumph that would follow.

The odours of blood were creeping into the tight, close chamber, but amidst the bustle and anxious shouting amongst the women, there finally came the thin and wavering cry of a new-born child.

"God be praised!" cried the midwife loudly. "A Dauphin for France!"

Margaret stole away.

"God be praised indeed," she muttered to herself. "I shall be freed at last."

Later that day, as if to confirm it, she heard the other news she had been anxiously awaiting. Her mother had made peace with Warwick.

* * *

Suddenly the silent and steady way of life at Amboise was at an end. The castle thronged with courtiers and knights and a sea of soldiers and servants. Noise and bustle everywhere. Great personages began to arrive for the double ceremonies of a christening and a wedding: the King and Queen of Sicily, the King of France, the whole clan of the Warwicks and finally, of course, Margaret of Anjou and Prince Edward.

The Queen was very quiet and her attire looked sombre considering the occasion. But she allowed the Warwicks to greet her without showing anger; she even made some effort to kiss the bride, Anne Neville, on the cheek.

Margaret welcomed her hopefully, taking care not to be effusive.

The Queen nodded to her, eyeing her narrowly.

"I trust I find you well, madame," said Margaret.

There had been no reply, and the Countess found herself continually trembling as she stood at her mother's side throughout the twin ceremonies. First the christening of the child, then the marriage. Prince Edward came to the altar in gleaming cloth-of-gold joining hands with the pretty, flushed Anne. The bride looked a little overwhelmed by the exalted company of so much royalty, high-born though she was. A shy girl was Anne, not wearing the magnificent silver bridal robes with any sense of presence. She was interested only in Edward, whom she loved.

The marriage was done: the procession formed behind the bridal couple to proceed from the chapel to the massive feast in the great hall. Now there was only Margaret left to walk behind the Queen of England and she could feel the Queen's boiling resentment all the time. No doubt much of it was directed still towards the smoothly smiling Warwick, but so was much of it intended for her unwelcome daughter.

"Madame—" she tried to appeal to the Queen again as

they came to a brief halt while the doors to the feast were flung open with a flourish of trumpets—"madame, can you not forgive and be peaceable to me?"

The Queen looked at her like flint.

"I didn't want you," she snapped, "and I will not change. You will bring bad luck, not good, as you tried to persuade me. You spoke of curses, daughter, and they are not lifted. Not from your father, not from any who touch the Lancaster cause—your fine Robin of Wakefield included."

Margaret flushed. She felt frightened inside; her mother was said to have the extraordinary gifts of a prophetess. She felt forced to fend her off.

"I shall not discuss Robin of Wakefield. He is amongst those who would free my father!"

"Bah," said the Queen forcefully, "only death will free your father! And think on this, only death will free you!"

Suddenly, everything was slipping away. A great blackness was coming down over Margaret and she was sliding to the floor in a welter of purple and gold damask. Voices cried out; there was shouting that surely came from miles away. Her face hit the cold flagstones and it was only for the shortest moment that she was aware of a pair of strong arms trying to pick her up.

Of the remainder of the wedding celebrations of her brother, the Countess would see no more.

* * *

When she opened her eyes again it was to stare straight into Robin's anxious face. She groaned and lifted one hand to her head. It felt as though it was about to split in two.

"Holy God," she said. "What happened to me?"

He lay down beside her without comment and took her into his arms.

"This will not do," muttered Robin. "To be apart. It is too great a pain."

"Ay," she laughed mirthlessly, quietly. "I've proved that. But I have had no choice."

"I knew it, lady. And that you wished only to please the Queen of England."

"Robin?" Margaret turned her head towards him, eyes bitter. "I see now that I shall never be able to do that. She has given me all yet she has given me nothing."

"Then you must cease to seek it of her further. Be strong. I am here and I worship you."

"You ought not to do that. I am going to return to my husband."

"Not yet."

"I wrong you foully," she said wretchedly. "Shall I tell you something, my lord of Wakefield? Your little whore was more honest a lover than I."

"I know you have used me," said Robin tautly. "For a release for yourself. In the hope of a child. For a dozen reasons, perhaps. But in the beginning you wanted me, loved me. I still think you do."

"If I do, then it is not enough. Not what you deserve."

"I shall be the judge of it," he retorted, seizing her into his arms. "Come now, will a Princess of England give me her body? Or must I take it?"

"I could have you hung for that now." She was mischievous with him for the first time. But it was soon gone.

Instead she threw herself into an interlude of wildly

enthusiastic love-making, all the more enjoyable for their recent parting.

* * *

The tidings had come speeding across the Channel to France: King Edward was in full retreat. The country was in the flames of revolt against him, and his party seemed doomed. He had only evaded capture by Lord Montague because one of his minstrels had warned him of his danger.

With Richard of Gloucester and Hastings and only eight hundred men, the King had dashed for his life towards the port of Lynn. He had hardly a gold piece, nor a velvet cloak left for his back.

The final, wonderful word was brought to Warwick at Calais.

"Edward of England has flown to Flanders. England awaits Lancaster."

Warwick sprang into frenzied activity. His moment had come. He called Clarence and Oxford into close conference; he sent out word for all possible troops to be brought to the muster.

"We move now!" he announced. "Now, without waiting for Queen Margaret. We shall cross to England and secure London—free King Henry, before any new resistance can spring up. The Queen can follow with the bulk of the French troops. By God, if only she had given her consent to ally with me before, we could have been ready, lock, stock and barrel."

Nothing could make it clearer what kind of war this had always been. Fortunes had swung so speedily from one side to the other that everyone had learnt to seize their immediate chance. Edward was gone. But for how long? Only a fool would imagine that he would not begin plotting at once in Flanders; striving to re-establish the army he had lost.

"God grant," said Oxford soberly, "that we shall have time then."

He did not like the shifty mien of Clarence at all. Of course it was this talk of freeing King Henry that did it. Duke George kept hoping Warwick meant the crown for him. Really the Earl was not very tactful.

"Is King Henry the right man?" Oxford demurred in an effort to put this right.

Warwick stared at him. Then he seemed to get the drift belatedly.

"Do you suppose the Queen would bring the troops for anyone else's support but her husband's? My lord, we want the men first. Securely on English soil. Then we can change our King. I suppose Henry will not object—for he has little life in him."

Did that mollify Clarence? It was to be hoped so. For there was no doubt that King Edward would be trying to win him back again now; the York brothers never allowed pride to stand in the way of necessity. It occurred to Warwick not for the first time, as it had already occurred to Richard of Gloucester, that it would be better for everyone if Clarence was dead.

Alas, fate never seemed to oblige; and there was no way a man dared to try and direct it himself.

"We sail within the week," Warwick announced now. "And march mighty quick across country. It's London we want, and I am going now to tell Queen Margaret so. Make way, my lords. And wish me luck."

* * *

Fickle England. There no longer seemed any stability of purpose in the common man nor any loyalty that lasted long. How was it possible to see rank after rank of cheering people greeting Warwick's ships and then his processions, as he made a steady way towards London? It was such a short time since they had been for Edward, almost to a man. Now they knew King Henry was to be restored and they were throwing the white rose badges from their caps wholesale.

Bells rang throughout the land, it was as though Warwick brought deliverance. His brother, Archbishop Neville, received him into the capital which had been his final destination: the seal on the new Lancastrian triumph. No more did Warwick practise secrecy in moving about the city, no more avoid Westminster. The palace was wide open to him, the courtiers who had chosen to remain were bowing and scraping to him, welcoming him with enthusiastic words and surely false smiles. What did they think of the weak and untrustworthy Clarence? Did they despise him as much as they probably despised themselves?

Trust, indeed, was not a word Warwick cared for. His landing and his *coup* of a royally deserted land had been almost too easy; he was looking anxiously for trouble. At once sending regular messages back to France to urge the necessity of swift reinforcements; Queen Margaret must not now dally.

To Clarence's disgust, the Earl now set himself up in his

favourite position: that of nominal King, real controller of the country. But he was uneasy: his spies watched at every port for any sign of Edward's return. He sent men to Flanders to watch over Edward's movements there, for it appeared obvious to Warwick that the Yorkist King would make an early effort to get support from his brother-in-law the Duke of Burgundy.

And in London itself there was plenty of other business. Edward's Queen had just fled into Sanctuary at Westminster with her children, and there she had borne a son. In the utmost terror of her life from Warwick and in the direst poverty. It did not move the Earl in the slightest.

"The babe that she has given Edward were best strangled," he muttered to Oxford darkly. "An heir for York—it is bad!"

The Queen cannot be taken from the house at St. Margaret's Churchyard," said Oxford warningly. "None would pardon it."

"Who is with her?"

"None but her immediate family and Lady Scrope."

Warwick grunted. Oxford was right there was nothing he could do, violating Sanctuary was far too heinous an offence. He would have to hope that Elizabeth Woodville would wait in vain for King Edward to return and be ultimately starved out of her refuge. Then, for her, and the princesses, a convent. For the boy—life imprisonment at best.

In the meantime there was another prisoner to think of, and my lord Earl gathered together an impressive deputation of noblemen and city dignitaries—who eyed him with some hardly veiled dislike despite their acceptance of him—and took the whole party by barge down river to the Tower of London.

The business, manifestly important though it was, did not take long.

Warwick was admitted into the Tower without question and the final select contingent marched briskly along in the company of warders to seek out the small and bare cell where the King who liked best to live as a monk had been held securely for upwards of eight years.

The Earl stopped before the thick oak door and peered eagerly in through the barred aperture. He saw what he expected, the tall and angular man seated at the rough table with his head of thinning fair hair bent over a book. Patient resignation in every line of his body.

"Open this door!" commanded Warwick in a loud voice that caused King Henry to jump up like a nervous hare, wide blue eyes staring fearfully towards his yet unknown visitors. The governor hastily obeyed with his own bunch of keys.

The Earl planted himself in the doorway at once, thumbs tucked into his belt. King Henry drew back.

"My lord King," Warwick addressed him then, and at last he bowed. "Don't look upon me like that. I have come to free you, to restore you to your own."

King Henry looked weak at the knees. He was sinking back on to his hard stool and shaking his head helplessly.

"Go away, my lord," he said faintly to Warwick. "Jests such as this cannot please me. Leave me in the peace I have taught myself to know—even in this place."

"It's true, my liege!" encouraged Oxford and the Archbishop. "You shall come back with us to your palace. Wear velvet again on your back and your own crown on your head."

Henry was utterly confused; there was no joy in him. Only distress. He quoted to them the lines of the poem he had written whilst in this gloomy cell as though he could think of nothing else to say.

"Kingdoms are but cares. State is devoid of stay."

"That may be, my lord King," said Warwick wryly. "But out you must come to face both of them once more."

TWELVE

Jasper Tudor had journeyed to France. Vastly changed from the sober and worried man he had been at Wynford. He sought Queen Margaret out at Calais, anxious to break the news that he had seen King Henry VI riding again in triumph through the streets of London.

"Banners flew," he told the Queen eagerly, "the conduits ran with wine and every man I saw, was wearing the red rose. There is none to withstand Warwick in England now."

"No," said the Queen dryly, putting a careful stitch into her tapestry, "there you are no doubt right, my lord. But tell me if the Londoners cheered my husband? Did they?"

"Ay, for sure they did."

The Queen looked astounded. Cheers for the Lancastrian in Edward's city? False, surely. But no matter, she would find real loyalty in the North and in Wales. She had been tirelessly assembling an invasion force in these last weeks, mustering the men offered by Louis. She was almost ready to embark for England.

"Daughter!" she turned imperiously to the Countess of Wynford who had appeared in the doorway, drawn there by the sound of Tudor's voice. "Bid the servants bring wine for my lord."

Margaret obeyed her quietly and then came in, making straight for Tudor's embrace. They said nothing to each other, but their affection was obvious. It irked the Queen for all she had rejected Margaret herself. Of course my lord of Pembroke would have been behind the advancement of a child always precious to him; yet she asked herself ridiculously now if she was a touch jealous? She had permitted the girl to rejoin her from Amboise; some pity had been aroused at last by her weary distress. But she kept her cold suspicions of Margaret's sanity, and indeed of her motives, well to the forefront; at best they had agreed on an uneasy truce. Her daughter's continued fornication with Robin of Wakefield aroused the Queen to helpless fury. For, whatever the girl's longing for her affection, nothing her mother said would part her from that man. She wondered if Tudor could succeed where she failed.

"Your uncle has brought good tidings," she told Margaret.

"I know," slowly, "I heard."

"So you are an eavesdropper are you?"

"I have often found it useful, Your Grace."

Damn the girl, she had a trip of the tongue that could set her mother back. Answer her in a way she understood all too well.

"You had best be respectful," snapped the Queen, "or I shall suggest a further visit to Amboise."

Margaret bowed her head but gave the distinct impression that she would have done so for no one else.

"Where is the Earl of Wynford?" the Queen was demanding. "Has he no care for his royal wife?"

That was certainly a sneer, and could only be an inference to Wakefield.

Tudor shrugged and this time he was gazing full at Margaret. He understood.

"My lord awaits the return of his wife eagerly. He assumed

she will come in your train, Your Grace, and plans to meet you in Kent. For the present he is busy mustering arms. Edward is said to be employed on the same bent in Flanders."

The Queen paled. The needlework was dropped. From outside could be heard the beginnings of what was to prove a succession of wild autumn gales and it was as though her system of premonitions was in action again.

"What special word from Warwick then?" she demanded.

"Only that he wishes most anxiously to see you in England, madame."

* * *

Margaret had made her deferential curtsey and gone out. Tudor found her leaning moodily on the parapet overlooking the harbour. The wind was gusting round the battlements and whipping a fine, flying spray from the sea beyond.

He glanced about him before he spoke.

"He knows," he said at last. "Richard knows."

"About my lord of Wakefield?" defiantly. "I supposed that he would."

"Why, Margaret? Now that you have almost everything you wanted?"

"Was he not instrumental in giving it to me? Were it not for him I should have stayed a virtual prisoner within Wynford."

"Then give him up now! The Earl will forgive you. He still loves you. By God!" Jasper smote one fist into the other angrily. "I tried to warn him but he would not listen! Yet I suppose he was right to let you go. And I rejoice to see you acknowledged as the King's own at last. But if you owe Wakefield so much, you ought to set him free now, not keep him tied to you like a lap-dog. For that is what I hear said, Margaret, short as the time is that I have been here. A lap-dog! A man like that. For shame, I say. I thought I knew you better."

"Stop," she said fiercely. "I will tell you something: I thought I knew myself better. But I begin to see I do not know myself at all. My lord—" the glance she turned on him was abruptly terrifying, desperate and dark—"the Queen hates me. Calls me daughter because she was finally forced into it, but hates me. She wants to destroy me. I believe she will succeed."

"Margaret—" Tudor groaned. "That is nonsense! She hates bending her will, that is all!"

"No, your soft talk cannot mollify. I know the truth. She is plunging me into agony. You see the way she speaks to me and treats me. I shall never be allowed to be the loving daughter I have longed to be. Nor indeed, the loving wife. For I recognise the truth at last; I don't love Richard. I don't love Wakefield. You understand? I have discovered that I merely need either one or the other to comfort myself. I am utterly selfish. Deny me any comfort at all and I would rather be dead. I have thought of that often, my lord—death."

A strange, wild look was directed now towards the tossing sea in the distance.

"A good leap out, my lord; a good one. I should crash to the ground and be beyond all hurt and all loathing of the way I am."

"For the love of God," protested Tudor in horror, "enough, Margaret!"

This was terrible; not since her early girlhood had he seen her looking like this. As though black demons tormented her within by the hour, as though the knowledge of her old rejections had merely been fuelled into new life by her new, once so cherished, contact with her mother.

"There is nothing wrong with you, Margaret," he said weakly.

Again that craving, frantic glance.

"It's not so. She knows it—the Queen! I saw it plainly written in her face and at last she has brought me to realisation. I have my father's morbid disease, my lord. One day the fits of madness will begin to rack me even as they do him. I shall be a poor, sad puppet, seated at Wynford's table. Even my memories will have deserted me. And you deny me Wakefield's love now! Bah!" She snapped her fingers at him. "You, and my mother. She is not above the dropping of her hints. Loth to own me, but equally loth to see me lie with Robin Wakefield. I do not care."

"You must care!" said Jasper, thinking wildly of the plans he had whispered of to Wynford. Did he dare to drop a hint, distract her? "One day England might need you."

"Me?" she started to laugh hysterically. It was a strange, loud and fanatical sound that suddenly sent shivers down Tudor's back. For the first time in his life he retreated from her and left her alone on her exposed parapet, with the wind blowing her hair out like a copper cloud about her head.

* * *

Three times in the coming five months, Queen Margaret was to strive to cross the raging Channel with her ships.

Those precious ships that were bringing baggage, soldiers and supplies to augment those amassed by Warwick and his allies. In England the Earl waited with ever-growing anxiety. He had London and he had the King; he had Elizabeth Woodville still penned up with her family as his hostages. But by the time the new year was bursting again into new life, Clarence had gone.

Disappeared as mysteriously from Warwick's side and allegiance, as a spectre by night, back to his brother. Was there really no end to his perfidy? Warwick felt himself panic a little. This was bad. All his high hopes and aspirations had never permitted him to feel over-secure and here was Margaret still delayed, no doubt in a fuming ferment on the other side of the Channel. By March the gales had begun to abate at last.

It released the Lancastrian fleet from Calais Harbour. It did more. It released the horrifying extent of Edward's new fleet from Flushing. With two thousand well-armed men at his disposal, the Yorkist King sailed over without mishap to make a landing at Ravenspur.

"We are undone," said Warwick grimly to his brother, Lord Montague. "God forgive me if I lie down before I am beaten. But I feel this is the end for us and for King Henry also. Margaret cannot now get here in time."

"What do we do?" asked Montague wearily. Like the Earl he was already in full armour, his men at the ready in the palace and in the city. London bustled with military might. Yes, and with excitement. They smelled a return of their favourite and were not afraid now to show it. King Henry sat silently on the throne he had briefly been given back, still lost in some mournful world of his own. He might just as well have been back in the Tower for all he appeared to care.

"Fight!" cried Warwick fiercely. "What else? Though we lay down our lives, we shall never give Edward a reason to jeer at us. I made him what he is. He must never forget that."

The Earl had left his family behind him. His Countess, his daughter Anne. If it hurt to think afresh on Isabel's new defection with her husband, it was useless to pore over that now. He would probably never see any of them again.

Warwick marched out of London in April, riding at the head of a stolid, silent and grim-faced army. It wound its way through the narrow streets almost like a funeral procession, banners flying. The bear and ragged staff, the star of Oxford.

As soon as the last of the massive army had gone by and the final, lumbering baggage cart, someone started to toll the bells of London.

From St. Paul's to St. Cross, from All Hallows to St. Mary Undercroft, the great sonorous clangour began to echo and to swell. The whole city seemed convulsed by noise. Yet there was no instinct for cheering. They knew Edward had come back, that he was possibly marching to meet Warwick even now, but they would have to wait until they had the final news of Edward's new triumph before they went mad with joy.

It would prove to be on Easter Sunday, 1471.

* * *

"Barnet?"

Blanche had roused herself from the couch where she

had fallen asleep. She looked particularly beautiful with the rosiness of slumber still about her, her pale green eyes lazy. She sat up and put back her rumpled yellow hair, frowning. The noise was frenetic out in the city; now the bells were ringing with a paean of triumph, and not just for Easter. This was quite different from the spine-chilling, funereal tolling, which had followed Warwick's departure.

"Ay, Barnet!" proclaimed Master Cartwright, respected city alderman, happily. "Warwick's dead, my dear. Montague too. It's the end for the King's enemies."

Blanche felt oddly bewildered. It was often that way with her these days. She had found her refuge easy enough to come by, returning to her old way of life since Edward's flight. In these past months she had moved from rich man to rich man, though of course no one compared with a king. But perhaps she had learnt something in that time. Kings were not to be relied on, nor trusted. Edward had offered her no real protection when she was afraid. And she was still afraid of Robin. But very often she told herself now that she deserved to be, that she had treated him shamefully and indeed that if she had ever loved anyone, it was he.

Once rejoicing at this news would have been simple for they had both been on the same side. But she had driven him to Lancaster. He might even have been at Barnet; he might be dead.

"Was it a great slaughter?" she asked faintly of her protector.

By the Mass, this kind of life was not really what she had believed it to be after all. A noble and kind man had been more than ready to marry her. Could she go on being a plaything for ever? She had begun to remember how her mother Germaine du Bellay had ended—ugly and alone. Even accused of witchcraft by old Beaufort's servants. Some said that by her demise Germaine had escaped the stake just in time.

"Ay, my dear. Great. All Warwick's baggage train captured they say. Queen Margaret will find a mighty poor welcome awaiting her in England now. But I suppose she will still come. A harpy of a woman. I like them soft and loving such as you, Blanche."

She could suddenly have spat at him for the clawing touch of his gnarled but still lustful hands. She could have been sick to think of him again possessing her body. But what was the use?

* * *

A week later King Edward re-entered his capital once again. Wretched King Henry VI was back in the Tower, but placed this time under a heavy guard of which he had in the past years been relieved. But it did not seem to bother him unduly, any more than had his all-too-brief return of Kingship. Perhaps, unstable in his mind as he was, he had even seen more clearly than Warwick in the very beginning—that the triumphant new rule of Lancaster had been far too tenuous. And that England was still completely unpredictable. Much as they had grown to resent Edward they had certainly resented the dominance of Warwick more. That was why the golden son of York had been able to come back and win over friends once more. For the final time. The people had chosen permanently between White and Red Rose at last.

Grinning, waving, Edward rode through the brilliantly

bedecked streets and heard the roars of approbation ringing from the river up to St. Paul's. Beside him rode his tearfully smiling and relieved Queen, just brought out of Sanctuary with the babe Edward in her arms, and her daughters clinging to her skirts. Elizabeth Woodville was a very lucky woman and she knew it, only her flight to the protection of St. Margaret's had saved her from Warwick. Behind the King were Richard of Gloucester and George of Clarence. It was quite remarkable how the latter Duke kept up his face when everyone knew what a double-dyed traitor he was. Certainly the scowling Gloucester had no use nor kindnesses for him, he even rode his horse further apart from Clarence's than need be.

But, exultant at the head of his procession, Edward paid no heed at all. He had what he wanted at last, he was an undisputed King.

At Westminster, Hastings was waiting for him. He did not look as happy as he should have.

"It's not over," he told Edward as the King and Queen seated themselves smiling on their twin thrones. His voice was almost lost in the splendid blast of the trumpet. "Margaret's fleet has set sail from France. The Prince of Wales is with her."

Edward glared at him, waving an elaborately gloved hand at the squalling child in the Duchess of Bedford's arms. Cicely of York was looking sour because the Queen's mother held the child.

"Prince of Wales, my lord? *There* is the Prince of Wales. Please remember it."

"Your pardon, my liege. But I need not stress that Queen Margaret will never allow that to be so. And the Prince has married Warwick's daughter to make matters worse.

There is only one possible solution."

"Of course," murmured Edward. "And God grant we shall be sent it."

"The army must march on Margaret, Sire. You have triumphed but the annihilation must be final."

"All must die," growled the Duke of Gloucester. "All!"

Clarence thought: now is the time I should make free with the knowledge I gained in France. Tell them of the Countess Margaret. But no: why should I? They have not treated me as they ought to have done since I returned to their banner, let them wait a while longer for my confidences. Edward owes that to my brother Richard's sour face.

Thus, although he had once boiled with enthusiasm to speak of the Countess, he exchanged a meaning glance with Duchess Isabel who certainly did not appear to be mourning her father overmuch; and spitefully continued to hold his peace.

THIRTEEN

For sixteen days, the Lancastrian fleet had been fighting its way over the Channel, a passage which should normally have been completed in twelve hours. The travellers were sick and wretched, often near to despair. It did indeed seem that Margaret of Anjou was accursed, especially when it was known that Edward had landed in England safely. The time was a torture. For Countess Margaret, still kept firmly at arms' length by her mother and daily looking wilder and more tormented in the mind. For Robin, who could see with dawning horror the truth of what was happening to this magnificent woman he had come to adore. Jasper Tudor saw it all too plainly in his turn, and it could only seem like the crassest folly that he should start muttering to Robin of the possibilities already discussed with Wynford —that this beautiful creature who was no longer normal should one day be considered as Queen.

"Stop, my lord," Robin had cursed at Tudor as they clung together to the heaving rail of the ship. "Stop! You are the madman! You would not dare broach this to Queen Margaret!"

"For sure I would not," retorted Tudor. "I know better to bide my time."

"The Countess is ill! She knows that for herself! God help me, if I could only do something to ease her agonies!" Robin slammed one fist into the other. "But I cannot! Her foot is set fast on the treadmill and I believe we are all responsible for it, in one way or the other."

"Then you knew not the Countess Margaret," snapped Tudor. "Deranged or not, she always followed her own mind. And if she keeps one, will do that to the end."

* * *

The Lancastrian ships had crept into Weymouth at last, battered and broken. The crews were bedraggled and exhausted, desperately in need of dry clothing and good food. The Queen chose to make quickly for the shelter of the abbey of Cearne with Prince Edward, Princess Anne and the Princess Margaret.

They had scarcely had time to settle themselves in and take meat before men came battering on the doors of the abbey, demanding entrance for my lady the Countess of Warwick and for my lord the Earl of Wynford.

Margaret had risen to her feet, going very pale. She went herself to the door and tugged it open; at once Wynford's starkly accusing face was confronting her. She could find no words to greet the man she knew she had betrayed. But Lady Warwick was giving no chance for private quarrels to have an airing; with despairing force she was pushing past both Wynford and his Countess and approaching the Prince of Wales and Queen Margaret. The Queen pulled herself up from her couch with a look of frozen horror on her face.

"By God," she said to Warwick's wife, "there's death writ on you."

The Countess of Warwick broke down, the floods of bitter tears bursting forth, and she wept as though she would never stop. Anne of Warwick had run to her, throwing her arms round her mother-in-law's shoulders.

"Oh my lady," she was whispering imploringly, "what is it? You must tell us!"

But the Countess could not. It was left to the Earl of Wynford to approach the Queen grimly. He had not looked again at the trembling Margaret.

"Your Grace," bitterly, "go back to France. Escape while you may."

The Queen shrieked.

"Go back? Go back you say? What talk is this, by the Cross?"

"Madame, the Kingmaker is dead and buried—slain at Barnet field. Thousands of his men and yours with him. That is what we have come to tell you. You cannot have enough support left in the land! Be warned, and flee!"

"Montague?" she asked hoarsely. "Not Montague!"

"Dead also. I tell you it is finished, madame."

Queen Margaret was slipping slowly to the ground, unconsciousness overcoming her. At once it was her daughter, fiercely protective, who had swept everyone else from her path and run to her mother's side. She shook her head furiously at the Prince and Princess of Wales as they would have taken the Queen from her.

"No. Leave off from her. It is only while she cannot fight me that she would lie still in my embrace. Have the mercy not to deny me that!"

They drew back, very solemn, and Richard Wynford noticed it at once. Noticed, despite the calamity of the occasion, that something was deeply different and wrong with the wife he had parted with in hope and trust. He had come here ready to accuse her of adultery with my lord of Wakefield who so far had not presumed to show his face though he knew he must be here at Cearne. For did not all men say Wakefield was never very far away from my lady of Wynford? It had become a sneering jest, fit to turn a man's stomach. It did not help for Jasper Tudor to say "I told you so."

"Margaret?" The Earl spoke sharply, in real agitation

Holy God, what was that wildness in her eyes? Still beautiful but filled with an inner agony and conflict he could not even begin to understand. He hardly recognised her.

"You too, my lord," her voice vibrated with anger, "leave off in your turn. You shall not draw me away until I am ready."

"You are my wife," loudly. "Where is your greeting for me?"

"I am a Princess," she retorted. "My loyalty is first to the throne and my mother. I shall make that plain."

Baffled, furious, Wynford turned on his heel and strode out. It was more than unfortunate that he should almost bump into Robin at the door. Too much for him.

"God's eyes!" he bawled at him. "What a fool I was! Have you tumbled my wife so often you have divested her of her sanity?"

Robin, cold, wanted to shout that it was more than his advent that might have done that. Or had it simply been the truth all along and none had known it, not even the Countess herself? Only the Queen, whose astonishing insight had never failed her, had not been dissuaded.

"It is the Queen who is to blame," muttered Robin at last, pushing past. "She has given her all but witheld all. The Duchess was not strong enough in her wits to withstand that. My lord—God's face, I don't want to say it because do what you will to me, I love her. But she never was strong enough. And now I think it is too late."

"What, for the grace of Heaven, are you saying?" Wynford asked hoarsely.

"You know, my lord Earl," wearily. "You have just seen it yourself."

And Robin, forgetting any courteous bow, had gone away.

* * *

That night he sought the Countess out whilst she lay alone in the darkness on her fur-covered couch. There was not even the friendly light of a candleflame in the cold bare room. She knew the moment he entered by the soft rustle of the curtain but did not so much as turn her head. Margaret was lost again in the great slough of darkness that had begun to encompass her mind so much of late; a darkness which emanated from some bottomless pit she could never fathom. It robbed her of emotion, almost of thought; it made her weak like some vile, wasting disease.

"My lady?" Robin whispered penetratingly.

"Ay."

"I saw you seek your rest alone."

"The Duke has gone," very low. "But you must know that. He has ridden off to join with my lord Somerset and Jasper Tudor. They think to raise fresh help for my mother and my brother."

He had found his way to her side and without asking, stretched out beside her. But when he put his arms around her it felt as if he was embracing a statue and the cheek he kissed was like marble.

Robin cursed. He sat up.

"So that's it. I should have known! Once back in England you are Wynford's again."

"You misjudge me then," hollowly, "for the truth is, I am no man's."

"Margaret! Don't yield to dismay."

"I am ill," wretchedly. "In my head. Like my father. It is the curse Katharine the Fair brought from France, the curse of the Valois. The Queen is right to hate me and I was wrong to force myself upon her. I see it now."

"After this," he said hoarsely, "you are going to forbid me to touch you."

"On the morrow we travel to Beaulieu," she said. "There to wait until my uncles have news to encourage us to march."

"March! Shall you go with them? You?"

"It is my place, is it not? That, I cannot be denied."

"And what of me?" grimly. "Am I to be denied?"

"No," she sighed and he could tell that she forced herself this time to open her arms and receive him into her embrace. By God, it had felt like touching a statue and now it was like loving a statue, somehow obscene.

He left her before any completion of their union and she did not try to call him back. There were tears in his eyes as he sought out a place amongst the other knights around the central fire in the hall. It was as he had told Wynford: he still loved her and no doubt he always would. But the copper-haired enchantress had finished with him. He had lost her as surely as he had lost Blanche la Belle.

Blanche! Where was she now, he wondered. Starving perhaps. Even dead? Had Warwick's men perhaps found and killed her, knowing what she had been to King Edward? By the Mass, had Robin himself been often more than a little unkind in the way he had remembered her and cursed her in the past?

Well it did not matter any more. Nothing did.

* * *

On Tewkesbury Field, Lord Somerset had made the decision to bring the army to a halt. Now, by the beginning of May, the Welsh lords had been persuaded to augment those French troops of Queen Margaret, with several tough companies of foot soldiers and archers. Persuasions had lured the Lancastrian royal family out again to the march; Prince Edward was more than ready for battle.

So was Edward the King, who had brought his own force up speedily from London, and who was now encamped less than a mile away. Once more the opposing sides of Red and White Rose were poised for battle but few really doubted the outcome, even though Queen Margaret rode up and down the lines of her men rallying them with her encouragements and promises of reward if they won the day.

The sun rose as a hard red ball into the heavens; the shrilling of the trumpets began. The steady drum of a hundred coursers' hooves was shaking the earth; nearer and nearer converged the two forces. Standards waving, broadswords brandishing, hoarse voices yelling battlecries.

"An Edward! Edward, Prince of Wales!"

"Edward, King of England! Death to all his foes!"

With an almighty crash the two armies had come together. Coursers reared, swords hacked at ringing shields and heavy armour and knights fell from the saddles to be trampled underfoot on the grass which soon turned slippery with blood. Men fought like maddened creatures everywhere, hewing and cleaving. This was desperation; the final strife and all of them knew it. No quarter could be asked or given. The Prince of Wales was young, some thought almost womanlike in his looks, but he proved today that he was no flinching Henry VI. Bold, almost fanatical, he strove mightily with the best that York could muster against him. But he had no skill as a general; he was forced to rely on Somerset and Lord Wenlock for that. What vile mischance was to lead to the misunderstanding between those two in the midst of the battle, the Prince would never know. Only that Somerset finally lifted his great battle-axe up and dashed Lord Wenlock's head in two. At once blind panic ran through the Lancastrians, for they could not understand what was happening. What kind of fight was this when their leaders put each other at such little value? Wenlock's men started running. The gap they left behind them was all too wide.

"Come back!" Robin heard the Prince screaming in rage. "Come back, traitors!"

It was no use. The numbers were unequal in seconds and Edward's men were pushing forward hard; overrunning the Lancastrian defence. Robin saw the Prince of Wales smote from his courser, to crash into the bloodied mire and lie still in his heavy suit of armour. From somewhere he could also hear Queen Margaret's frenzied screaming before Somerset presumably went so far as to have her dragged forcibly away from the carnage. He saw Edward the King dismounting from his horse and tramping up to the fallen Prince, stirring him with his foot as the noise and madness of the battle started to retreat. Gloucester had followed him; he was wrenching the beaten Prince to his feet where he swayed crazily. His helmet had fallen off and his blond hair was blowing wildly in the breeze. Somehow he was staring with fury at the King who had stolen his throne.

"I will ask you why you came here!" bawled the older man.

"To recover my father's crown!" yelled the Prince. "And my own inheritance!"

The King struck him violently across the face with his gauntlet: in a trice several men had fallen upon the Prince with their sharp daggers and Gloucester made sure he was one of the first to strike deep. The heir of Lancaster fell choking on blood to their feet, lying there to twitch slowly into death.

* * *

Robin, hiding amongst the wounded, waited with bated breath until the royal murderers had passed by, the Prince's body borne before them on a hastily summoned litter. This field of Tewkesbury was a terrible place now, littered with the dead and dying. Screams and groans assailed Robin's ears; he felt as though he was in hell listening to the tortured damned. Full many a battle he had seen but none so bloody and foul as this. It looked as though half the men and coursers of England had met a grisly end here today. Somehow he pulled himself away from the bodies with which he had protected himself; he could smell blood thick on his armour and it made him want to retch. But apart from minor sword-thrusts, he was himself unharmed. Despite exhaustion, he could begin to creep on all fours through the piles of bodies and crawl his way in this fashion from the field. His sense of direction remained good although darkness had begun to fall before he had gone far enough to dare to stand and stare, panting, about him, seeking in the growing gloom for the path that led from the fields into the copse of a wood and then to Tewkesbury Park—the house where he guessed Queen Margaret had been taken. But care was needed. In the distance he could begin to see the first flares of the torches carried by King Edward's men as they began to search the surrounding district for runaways from the battle so that they too could be put to death. They would be kicking down doors and probably setting fire to barns.

Robin began to run. He stumbled twice into muddy ditches and into piles of straw; his face was scratched and bleeding again: he knew he must stink like a pig. But there, at last, was the house. With no light in any of the windows, it looked quite deserted. Of course, it would. He stumbled up to the big door and began to knock softly on it; the signal that ought to convey that he was a friend.

"Hurry!" he was hissing at last as the door was opened a stealthy crack. "It's Robin of Wakefield! Take me to Her Grace at once!"

There was a rough order, given in the Earl of Wynford's voice and the door was pulled open at last. Robin found himself hauled forcibly inside, Wynford glared down at him. A fearsome sight, filthy, bloody.

"What have you to say?" he demanded harshly, shaking Robin by the arm. He ought to have resented it, but somehow he did not. The Earl's agitation was too real.

"The Prince of Wales is dead. Killed by Gloucester and divers others, my lord. And the Queen is being sought for, even now."

"Holy Face!" The Earl's eyes seemed to retreat into his head with horror. He crossed himself, great gauntleted hand over his thick breastplate. Somerset had come up at the back of him, speechless.

"This is the end," said Wynford finally, his voice broken. "The end! This news will kill the Queen."

"For sure if we do not get her away from here, Edward's men will do it instead in the mood they are in!" Somerset cried then. Like the others, he could hear the advance of the noisy search through the woods outside. There was but the scantest chance for Margaret of Anjou and Anne Neville to escape.

"My lords, they are safer kept here!" Robin was protesting violently. "They can be hidden. Let the scum vent their wrath on our bodies if they must and so be contented! This house must be full of secret places."

Somerset would not hear of it. He saw only the plain duty of getting Queen Margaret away and himself with her.

"Wynford!" He had pushed Robin aside and that with the least of respect as though he meant nothing and this time resentment did spring up, for it was uncalled for. "We go to the Queen and the lady Anne; your wife, also. There is still time to slip from the back of the house and ride for Coventry. We shall not tell her of the Prince's death, or I think she will not move from here. Remember—the King still lives."

He strode off into the darkness of the house to bring out the hidden Queen; but as the Duke of Wynford would have followed him, Robin leapt forward and grasped his arm.

"My lord, listen to me! Leave your lady here. I swear

to protect her with my life. I can take her back to your castle, back to the protection of Jasper Tudor. None of Edward's men yet know of her; she will be safe if only she does not run!"

"Ay," said Wynford suddenly. "By God's body, you're right. Let it be then. But I must go with Somerset and the Queen."

* * *

Within the half-hour, the exhausted Margaret of Anjou and Anne Neville had crept out of the house, heavily cloaked, and found their way to swift horses. Somerset, Oxford and Wynford went with them. Not even the faintest flicker of a torch could light their way and even the light of the moon coming from behind a cloud was to be dreaded.

Robin was left alone to contend with the unbridled fury of the Countess whom he had kept behind.

"You cur!" she screamed at him. "This was your doing! Were it not for you the Earl would have taken me too! You have separated me from my own! I would rather have died at the Queen's side! You want to take me back to that prison—to confine me again from Edward, just as I was once confined from my mother!"

"Lady, I think you do not understand!" raged Robin. "Your brother is dead and your father's life will surely soon be forfeit! That leaves only you. The heiress of noble Lancaster. Ask your uncle, my lord of Pembroke, when you see him. Ask him if he is not determined what that shall mean."

By the Mass, why had he been fool enough to say that?

Not even driven by desperation to keep her quiet, should he have done so. That terrible, mad scheme of Pembroke's; it did not bear thinking about. Margaret Queen? Queen Regnant of England? Not fully in her wits, but absolutely under the control of powerful and dangerous men who would use her even though their cause lay trodden in the dust? She would be destroyed. All hope of her safety would be gone. She was a woman, but that would not stand in King Edward's way.

But there was no backing out now. She had fallen utterly silent, staring at him. The enchantress' eyes were filling with awe; then beginning to glitter strangely with pride. She held herself suddenly very straight.

"Our Lady," she murmured at last, "can it be? I who was nothing, to be turned into all? No dream of mine could ever have surpassed it."

Robin was taking hold of her shoulders and bundling her before him. There were lights bobbing about outside, the tramp of feet and the shout of voices.

"Move, for God's sake!" he whispered furiously. "Move, else we are done for!"

He pushed her into the secret place where her mother had been, and squeezed in after her. The space was hot and confined; he prayed they would not be left there long, as he closed the panel after them. Already he could hear Edward's men breaking down the door and beginning to surge into the house. Their shouting re-echoed, and they were everywhere, tearing down hangings, breaking open chests and cupboards. Beside him, Robin could feel Margaret trembling, but he no longer dared to reach out for her hand to comfort her. She was beyond all that. Had she not already made it plain that he was nothing now but a servant? Thank God, it had actually begun to lose some of its sting, though he cared immensely still for her safety; her death would wound him sickeningly and he could not be sure he would recover. Or indeed that it would be significant if he did not.

"There are none here!" came the fiercely relieving cry at last. "None! If the Queen has been here she is long fled."

"Ay, give it up! We must needs look further afield for our quarry."

Robin's skin prickled. He knew that voice was Richard of Gloucester's.

"Hurry," it went on, "the King wants to make good speed for London again. Ay, myself also. I believe I have pressing business there."

The cold hard laugh that followed that might have meant little to Margaret, but Robin thought at once of quiet, placid King Henry, and his heart sank with pity.

The search party was quitting the house; they could be heard tramping away. At once Robin was on his feet, cursing his cramped limbs, pushing open the darkly confining panel and hauling Margaret out after him.

"Now," he said. "Are you ready, lady? We have much speed to make on a long and hard journey. With luck yonder fellows have left off their searching and we may find horses in due course—but until then we are on foot."

"I can keep up with you," Margaret responded with dignity. She seemed far away from him. He guessed miserably that she was dreaming of a crown, and it was going to be difficult enough simply to get her back to Jasper Tudor without her being captured on the way.

* * *

Unknowing of her daughter's progress and largely uncaring, the Queen had struck desperately for freedom towards the Midlands. Her ill-luck was to come to curse her again. Before the end of the month she was a prisoner and so was Anne; most of their escort dead. Only Somerset had made his escape. For the rest King Edward was able to view his prisoners with triumph at Coventry as Sir William Stanley brought them to him.

"Now," he said, "I can return to the city! And you, madam, will come with me. A captive in my train."

"God's curse bedevil you and all your family!" Queen Margaret screamed at him, her arms secured by his guards. "You, who have slain my son, shall lose your own to violent death! I call upon Heaven to hear me and grant me that reward!"

"Silence the woman!" bawled Edward, who could not understand the sudden chill the Queen's words brought into the pit of his stomach. "In God's name silence her!"

She was dragged away, still raving. Edward felt weak.

"I ought to destroy her."

"Let me do it for you," said Gloucester eagerly. "Who has she left to defend her? Those that travelled with her are perished, save Somerset, and he will meet his just deserts soon."

"The Earl of Wynford is dead?" mumbled Edward. He wondered why Clarence started to move restlessly about the tent as though there was something he wanted to say, but didn't.

"I saw him slain myself," said Gloucester. "By the swords of two of my knights. Pity it is that Pembroke and Somerset had not been at his side."

"Ah well," said Edward in some relief. "He had no kin

to trouble me. So be it; he had goodly estates and they are now forfeit to the crown."

"What's the matter with you, brother?" demanded Richard of Gloucester in a surly voice of Clarence, noting the agitation in his turn.

"Perhaps it does not yet suit me to tell you!" Clarence sneered at last. He thought: this charade cannot last much longer. Only while King Henry still lives. After that I shall likely be slain if I don't tell the truth in time.

"I warn you—" began Gloucester, but Clarence actually sniggered at him and went out.

"He knows something," snarled Gloucester at Edward. "Beat it from him! It is important—I sense it! It is something he learnt whilst with Warwick."

Edward scowled.

"You know he is a fool."

"Brother, we must go to London. Delay no more!"

Edward averted his eyes. He knew perfectly well what must happen once he marched back into the city. Why, he wondered, should he now feel squeamish about necessity? Had he not fought for years to set himself free of Henry VI? He had let him live too long. While he lived there could never be security for his crown or his baby son. Yet to slay an anointed King—by the Mass, it made a man's flesh creep strangely. And brought some promise of a curse to come, akin to that of Queen Margaret.

Bah! He shook himself then. Was he to be that much afraid of a mere woman? A woman he would drag back now to London in ignominy, practically in chains, with Anne of Warwick beside her?

"We'll go," he said to Gloucester, "at dawn. With both the women."

The Duke's eyes narrowed with a sudden look of speculation. Even of interest.

"She is fair," said Gloucester, "Warwick's daughter. Very fair of face."

Edward stared at him.

"Keep your mind to business," he found himself saying in astonishment. "She is an enemy. And if she keeps any son of the Prince of Wales in her womb, she is doubly so."

Richard grunted sourly. Presumably he had been corrected, because he had drawn his dagger and he had begun to run a finger along the sharp edge of it. He was not likely to fail King Edward now.

FOURTEEN

The Tower of London lay in deep darkness. Mist from the river was creeping up its steep ramparts, with a chill fit to make the teeth chatter, and even the thickness of a cloak could not keep the rawness out. In the royal apartments carousing had been going on for several hours; a butt of red wine had been long since broached. King Edward and his brothers, had brought their captives into London in the triumphant early morning. Richard of Gloucester and his men had repaired to the ancient fortress almost at once and clearly meant to sleep there tonight. In her own miserable place of confinement in one of the towers, Queen Margaret now lay; Anne Neville in another, both frightened, weary women.

In his cold and cheerless cell, King Henry VI had stretched out on his own hard couch having said his prayers for several hours on his knees. He knew nothing of the arrival of his Queen, and nothing of the death of his son. The outside world simply continued to pass him by and he heeded it little.

He was almost asleep when he heard the first faint rattle at his door. He lifted himself up to stare towards it, seeing it open gradually with the chink of light widening behind it. Dark figures stood there, outlined ominously. He heard the steel slither of daggers leaving their jewelled sheaths.

"No!" cried the King, paralysed with terror. He flung

himself further away from them. "No! Holy Cross, protect me! You cannot kill me—I am God's anointed!"

But with a roar of laughter, the men leapt upon him and held his struggling frail body down. Blow after blow plunged into Henry's flesh until the blood was spurting everywhere and his screams were stifled under hard hands. At last they had finished and stood back; the limp body rolled from the couch and fell to the cold stone of the floor. Henry's hands still twitched spasmodically. He coughed horribly, choking on blood.

"That's the end of you, God's anointed," snarled the leader. "Good riddance to it."

Henry was whispering a last, faint prayer which no one heard.

"Holy Cross, receive me! Receive me!"

He was dead before the murderers went stealthily away.

* * *

There was already much renewed gaiety at Westminster. Messengers had to thread their way through dancing and gaming, through a mass of courtiers who had retrieved their old court finery and seemed ready to put all the traumatic events of the last years finally behind them.

There was even a fascinating new mistress in chief to be seen at Edward's side; Jane Shore, the goldsmith's wife, had come into her own at last. The King had eyes for no one else. The Queen appeared still to be too glad of her restored safety to indulge too much in jealousy. She had her crown back, and her importance.

Hastings carried the news to Edward.

"It seems there has been a mishap in the Tower," he

said. "King Henry is dead."

Edward was silent for a moment. He had expected this; but he crossed himself instinctively.

"God rest his soul," he said. "I ever pitied him."

Then he looked up. His eyes were gleaming, he took a deep breath.

"I'm free!" he pronounced. "God be thanked, free of all of them!"

He wondered why Clarence was coming forward with a sickly look on his face. He seemed to be finding it difficult to open his mouth.

"Well?" rapped Edward.

"I told you there was something it was too soon that you should know," mumbled the Duke. "But now the King is dead—it is time to speak."

"Time to speak of what?" bawled Edward, fright suddenly leaping on him again. The merrymaking in the hall had come to an end.

"You are not free," said Clarence slowly. "Promise not to kill me and I will tell you why."

"If you do not speak I shall kill you!" raged Edward, reaching out to shake the Duke by the shoulders. "God damn it, what do you know?"

"The Earl of Wynford," spluttered Clarence. "He had a wife none knew of! A child born to Queen Margaret long before the Prince of Wales and kept for long years by Jasper Tudor in secrecy! A Princess, brother. And now she is the heiress of Lancaster."

"Holy Face!"

Edward was on his feet, trembling. Gloucester had just come in and was gaping at him, not understanding the commotion where he had thought to see only rejoicing over his midnight deed in the Tower. But the King was scarlet, glaring down at Clarence as though he would have liked to see him murdered too.

"Why did you not speak before? Great God, so that we could have searched harder! This is beyond belief!"

"I swear it is true," quaked Clarence. "And Pembroke will use her."

"Of course he will use her!" bellowed Edward. "Christ's feet, we must find her! Throw her where she can do no harm, like her accursed mother! By the Mass—that woman! Will she never cease to curse me with her perfidy and her secrets? King Henry is dead but he was the guiltless one of the pair!"

Gloucester had come forward thunderstruck.

"It is as you say," he told Edward, "almost beyond belief. But now I see much: she was in league with Warwick. She was part of his plan to ally with the Queen. It almost succeeded but for fate being on the side of York. She will have escaped back to Wynford, Sire. There is nowhere else she could go, and Tudor would look to find her there."

"Shall I come with you?" muttered Clarence. "She will be well protected. Robin of Wakefield was always at her side."

Edward found it necessary to sit down. From scarlet his face had now blanched. Hastings, too, had caught his breath.

"Robin of Wakefield! By God, my lord, you have stood here times enough and heard us thresh our brains to know what had become of that traitor!"

"Well now you know," sullenly. " He was her lover. He went to Warwick first because the King took away the woman called Blanche la Belle. And then he fell under the

Countess' spell. You ought to know she is the most beautiful woman I ever saw."

"The devil she is," said Edward weakly. Good God, this was no time to feel a spark of interest in the female. She was his enemy. "I care nothing for it. She must be cast where she can cause no more trouble—at once!"

"To Wynford?" demanded Gloucester.

"Ay, by the Mass! By dawn-light."

* * *

For Jasper Tudor, who had been hiding since Barnet in his brother's castle at Caldicot, the supreme moment for decision had come. Tewkesbury had made an end of the Prince of Wales and the cause of Lancaster seemed utterly crushed. But for the Earl of Pembroke there could never be the final admission of defeat, especially when it was made known to him that his long-cherished Countess Margaret was still at liberty, thanks to the wits of Robin of Wakefield.

"All my life I dreamed she was worthy of the greatest reward," the Earl said to himself. "I will see a crown set on her brow."

Persuading a number of Edmund Richmond's men to join him and also several Welsh lords, Jasper set off at a good pace for Wynford where he knew he would find Margaret. Luck was to be with him, for Edward's advance had not yet begun from London and before he reached the castle, he had almost ridden into Somerset.

"Great God, my lord!" cried the Earl, confounded. "I did not think to find you here!"

"I am in peril of my life," said Somerset grimly. "The Queen was taken at Coventry."

"I know it. And King Henry has been slain in the Tower."

"How do we escape?"

"Across the mountains, my friend. In the lands of Wales there is safety for us all; protection until we can reach the sea."

"Harlech was taken!" protested Somerset.

"But my chieftains are still loyal to me," insisted Jasper. "And will be to my lady, whom they know I revere. Somerset—answer me now if you are in agreement with what I propose. Before we flee to fight another day, our cause demands a fresh rallying point. Are you with me?"

Somerset looked shaken. He would have been a fool not to guess what this fierce-eyed Welshman proposed, and by the look of the men with him, it would probably not be a good idea to resist him.

"The lady Margaret is all that is left," murmured Jasper meaningly. "Say you will take her, with me, to Worcester cathedral, and let her chaplain crown her Queen of England."

"But the danger of that!" said Somerset weakly, thinking he had just made one perilous escape simply to be plunged into fresh distress. And the lady Margaret to be crowned Queen? Surely no one else but Tudor would have suggested such a wild solution to the Lancastrian void. Nobles and knights never wanted to follow Queens. Had not Margaret of Anjou herself failed? "I think the Earl of Wynford would not have agreed to risk her life in that way," Somerset said at last. "For you know that is what you do—once you make her Edward's rival. As the Prince of Wales and King Henry have suffered, so shall she."

"You are wrong," gruffly. "The Earl would have consented. And I am here to shield her."

"You must ask her," said Somerset faintly. "At least ask her."

Slowly, the party, flying the Tudor banner, approached the massive walls of Wynford. Wakefield had defence well organised; the battlements bristled with armed men just as they had with the Earl in command. It was only after the most careful inspection that the Earls of Pembroke and Somerset were allowed to enter and plod their way through the succession of courtyards and gates. Curious throngs of soldiers and servants came out to stare, open-mouthed.

Robin had come out too, looking tall and broad-shouldered in his armour; clearly he spent every hour in anticipation of trouble in these once quiet foothills. The lady Margaret was behind him, staring at the new arrivals with an oddly glassy look about her eyes. Apart from that she was still at the very zenith of her fiery beauty, clothed magnificently in a flowing gown of purple velvet and silver lace.

Tudor and Somerset went forward to her and seeing their determination, the puzzled Robin moved to one side. The two Earls exchanged a glance. Then, as one, and with a concerted rattle of armour, they had both gone down on one knee in front of Margaret and bent their heads. The rest of their party followed suit.

Such was the sudden silence within the castle that the raucous cries of the ravens circling the battlements could be heard shrill and unchallenged.

"Your Grace," said Jasper Tudor, "accept the homage of your liege-men."

Margaret swayed a little, she put out a hand to Robin who seized it tightly at once. She hardly understood them. Why did they say 'Your Grace' to her? How could they?

"What is this charade?" Robin shouted angrily.

"It is no charade," said Tudor grimly. "The King is dead. Long live our Queen."

Margaret shrieked. She was crumpling up before their eyes, collapsing in another of the fits that came more and more often in these last days. Her father was dead; perhaps her mother too. It was too much. That they called her Queen would be more acceptable when she awoke again to consciousness. She would almost have forgotten Henry and would see herself anointed and wearing a crown that brought an almost childish excitement to the fore in her.

"By the Mass, this is ill done in you!" Robin was yelling over her inert body. "You cannot use her so! Don't you see that, between us, we have made her no longer what she was!"

Tudor looked stunned. He felt as if a blow had fallen on him. It was right then, she was no longer sane.

He squared his shoulders and rose to his feet with Somerset.

"I retract nothing," he said. "That woman is the Queen. I will see her crowned in this land before I take her to safety in France. Our day will come again."

Somerset was thinking privately that Tudor was as mad as his niece apparently was. He wanted desperately to side with Wakefield, but he knew, like Robin, that would only end by Tudor's men falling on both of them with their swords. They had no choice now but to follow his instructions.

FIFTEEN

Time was running out. Robin's spies had come spurring back to Wynford even as Pembroke was ready to set out on his journey, a dozen armed knights close about the lady Margaret's litter. Tight enclosed she was by the curtains, just as Robin had first seen her, and deathly pale. But taut with the strangest, inner exultation.

Like her uncle, she would not be moved by the news that King Edward and his men were well on the way towards Worcester.

"My lord, be warned!" the men pleaded, breathless, to Tudor. "If you take the road to the city now you are bound to converge! There is no hope unless you turn now and flee for Wales!"

"I will see the Queen crowned," gritted Jasper. "My arrangements are made."

They were indeed. A large bribe had persuaded the bishop to yield up his cathedral for the ceremony Jasper insisted upon. A farce of a coronation, with no royal crown, orb or sceptre, but he had found replacements for all of these and Margaret's chaplain was to set the crown on her head.

She peered out of her litter.

"I will be crowned," she said forcibly. "My uncle and I are as one."

Desperately, Robin tried to get near enough to beg her to change her mind. Or at least get her to consent to a ceremony in France. But he knew that would not do; Tudor had set her mind on Worcester.

"For God's sake then, let us make a start!" Robin shouted. "Or Edward will catch us before we ever reach the altar with the Queen."

Queen. He had never called her that before. Though she was some kind of queen amongst all women: a Red Queen. An emblem for destroyed Lancaster even as her fierce mother was left to rot in the Tower at Edward's mercy. What was to happen to Robin's Queen Margaret?

Death. This ghastly sinking sensation in the pit of his stomach was supplying the answer. He ought to be able to take her hand and mutter farewell, but he could not.

The procession moved out of the castle and turned to its journeying. Less than five hours would it take to Worcester, to the dangerous passing of the gates, even though Jasper Tudor had been busily bribing guards. It was not long since King Edward had passed this way after Tewkesbury, and Lancastrian faces would be known in their turn. But with colours concealed and helms fast down, the two Earls were able to pass and so were their men. No one challenged them at the West Gate; no one stirred the closed curtains of the litter.

"A sick woman," Robin muttered to a solitary questioner within the city. "She has the sweat and is near to death."

That was enough to make people shuffle back in haste, and, crossing themselves, to hurry away. When the litter was carried into the precincts of the cathedral they concluded it was her last request to perish in some holy place. No one came to investigate.

* * *

Margaret had emerged from her litter. She stared around her with awestruck wonder. For a moment her sad, listless brain was awake again, marvelling at the beauty of her surroundings, at the deep, incense-laden peace. Gold plate gleamed on the distant altar, candles gleamed. Her chaplain was coming slowly towards her down the long nave, a procession of monks bearing lighted tapers pacing behind him, chanting.

A coronation. That was what they had promised her.

Jasper Tudor had taken her left hand, and was nodding at Robin to secure the right. As he obeyed, she suddenly turned a smile of her old brilliance upon him and he knew with pain, that briefly she was herself again.

"Lead me then, my good friends," said Margaret softly. "I am ready."

She began to walk forward, steady and magnificent. She seemed to glitter from head to toe, so richly sewn with diamonds was the gold brocade gown and cloak. Ermine entwined her neck and the arms of her bodice; her copper hair was bound up tightly in a jewelled net. No one could have looked more like a real Queen.

They had reached the altar and the canopied chair which was placed before it. Tudor and Robin began to divest Margaret gently of the cloak and the net over her hair, and with its removal, the glory of her tresses tumbled down over her shoulders. She sat there with bent head, looking suddenly vulnerable. Her chaplain stood before her intoning prayers. A priest had brought a glistening bowl of sacred oil, and now the chaplain was anointing Margaret with it, on the head and on the breast. It was strangely moving to watch; and to hear her unsteady voice repeating age-old words her father must once have spoken before her.

"Je les graunt et promet—"

"Je le garderez—"

The chaplain was turning to receive the crown; to hold it over Margaret's head. Not the crown of England, but a magnificent double circlet nevertheless, gold and set with splendid rubies, chased with a design of *fleur-de-lis.* Tudor had spared no effort to bestow the best he possibly could upon his niece.

She looked up. Her fine eyes seemed suddenly and inexorably drawn to the glittering symbol poised above her head. She smiled. As the chaplain lowered the crown on to her brow, they saw her sigh as though she felt herself blessed by something infinitely sacred.

"God bless Queen Margaret!" whispered Jasper Tudor.

It should have been a mighty shout but they dared not make it that. Instead they must go almost in silence to kneel before her while the monks began a quiet version of Te Deum Laudamus. But subdued though it all must be, the deed was done. Crowned, the Queen sat enthroned before them, orb and sceptre now crossed over her breast. An image still as stone, dazzling the eyes, with myriads of candles dancing around her in the gloom. For a brief moment she seemed almost to mesmerise them, to imprint the vision of herself on their marvelling eyes for ever.

None of them had heard the distant tumult in the city, or the faint shouting and rattle of hoofbeats. Not even the spasmodic cheering.

* * *

Edward the King had brought his party spurring nearly up to the doors of the cathedral before he threw out his arm to halt them, to signal that they should hurl themselves from their saddles, and, swords in hand, creep stealthily after him up to the great main door.

Gloucester scuffed his foot on the cobbles and at once Edward turned on him, glaring, finger to his lips. Subdued sounds of Mass were drifting out from the old and beautiful cathedral, lingering on the sweet air of the summer evening.

"You see," Clarence was whispering, "it is as I told you it would be! Why else would Pembroke bring the woman here when he should be now have fled before us into his own lands?"

"Ay, he is a great traitor," muttered Edward, "and I'll have his hide for it."

They crept forward, and entered the cathedral, soft-footed as cats. Two of Tudor's men had been posted there as guards. It was violating a holy place but there was no help for it; Edward's strong hands and Richard's dagger had swiftly and efficiently disposed of both men: Clarence dragged them away. Now the way of entry was free.

The three brothers lifted the heavy curtain that blocked their view into the cathedral. And they stood there, speechless. The glistening creature who sat enthroned before the altar riveted their eyes, the splendour of her robbed them of movement. None of them had expected such a sight to blight their wits.

"God's eyes," whispered Edward at last, "but she is like the Queen of Heaven at Walsingham."

Margaret had seen them. Indeed, she was the only one to do so for the rest, Tudor, Somerset and Wakefield, had their backs turned to the door where the York brothers stood. Now was their moment: the instant to call in the rest of their men and overrun the nest of traitors and capture or slay them all. But the sight of the Red Queen had slowed Edward up. Margaret had time to rise to her feet; the expression of horror implanted on her previously serene face was enough to bring the other Lancastrians round, gasping, reaching at once for their swords.

That, at last, was the charm to release Edward from the spell.

"Traitors!" he roared into Worcester's echoing vastness. "Traitors! Take them all!"

He was charging forward down the aisle with Gloucester and Clarence, and their men had surged in, yelling, behind them. They converged on the party gathered round the altar with weapons hacking, slashing. Priests ran out to implore them to stop the carnage, to cease the sacrilege; it was useless. And for Edward, the delay in the attack was still to lose him his prizes; Somerset and Pembroke had somehow broken free and ran, heading for one of the side doors behind the altar. Margaret was left, with her back to the high table, the crown still glittering on her head. She was trapped, but quite magnificent, and that was how Robin would always remember her before he snatched his opportunity and raised his long dagger to point it at her breast. With all his strength he hurled it at her; the blade flew unerringly and plunged deep into her body. Coughing, choking on blood, Margaret was buckling at the knees and crumpling to the floor in the midst of her gold and bejewelled finery.

"Robin!" she screamed in bewildered agony. "Robin, why?"

She must know why. She must, he thought in anguish.

The fighting had stopped. There was not a man, including the stunned King, who had not turned to look as Margaret fell. And not a man but Robin of Wakefield who moved. He threw down his sword as though in disgust and went to her, kneeling by her side and cradling her in his arms.

Her beautiful eyes were full of agony and growing dim.

"God forgive me for what I have done," whispered Robin. "Margaret, forgive me. But I could not have let them take you, lady. To imprison you again, to heap humiliation upon you. I entreat you to understand. I loved you full well, Red Queen. Full well."

Odd: he used the past tense. Well why not? She was almost dead. Probably, when Edward had finished torturing him for what he had done, he would gain the mercy of death too.

She was struggling to speak, very faintly, but it was impossible. He would never even know if she forgave him. She expired in his arms as he knelt there. Robin laid her gently down and as he did so, he realised that two armour-clad and spurred feet had planted themselves firmly into his line of vision. The spurs were gold.

He didn't bother to look up.

"You can smite me down here if you wish, my liege," said Robin. "I do not care."

"No," gritted Edward. "I have been a-chasing of you far too long, my lord of Wakefield, to dispatch the business so fast. And you should have known of old that I like not those who deprive me of my prisoners."

At last Robin rose to his feet and faced him. Edward's blue eyes were like steel; there was no mercy here.

"As I," he said, "like not those who chose to deprive me of a wife."

Edward actually went scarlet.

"Secure this man!" he roared at his men. "Take him tight

and bind him!"

The guards rushed forward and laid rough hands on the prisoner, ready with the thick leather thongs to ensnare his arms. Robin cursed at them and struggled, but they had no trouble in beating him down. The King waved furiously that they should drag him away amongst the other prisoners.

"My liege," the monks were quaking at him now, "my liege, what have you done to God's house?"

"You may think yourselves lucky," snarled Edward, "that I choose to do no more! You have harboured traitors here, crowned a Queen! I should raze the place to the ground and hang you all high!"

Yet he was pushing them out of the way and going to stand over Margaret's corpse. She was perhaps not very lovely now, bloodied, her dead face creased in agony. But the King would never forget her as she had been when he had first walked through the door; he knew some part of him was already capable of forgiving Robin of Wakefield.

"Bury the lady," he ordered the frightened monks at last. "Secretly and with no mark over her grave. The world knew nothing of her, so let it remain."

And with his brothers at his side, King Edward went striding out of the desecrated cathedral. Within the hour he was taking his cartloads of fettered prisoners back to London.

* * *

Before dawn light, the monks of Worcester had buried the lady Margaret's body. With the maximum secrecy demanded of them by the King. The clods of earth were thrown back onto the makeshift coffin, and then they went away, already chanting a Mass for her soul.

They had buried her still wearing her coronation gown and her jewels; and amongst the rings on her fingers was the one Robin had given her. Nothing but a graceful willow tree would ever signify the grave.

SIXTEEN

Blanche la Belle saw the unhappy cargo coming back into the city, on its way to the Tower. She had been out in the streets, buying herself some new finery with Master Cartwright's money. It was not, of course, the sort of finery that the King had been able to provide, but somehow that no longer worried her as it had. Nor even did the sight of Edward himself, riding proudly on his fine white courser at the head of his soldiers. He was still the handsomest of men and probably the most pleasant to the ladies, and in the first days of his return, she had dared to hope he might seek for her. But she had been a fool, for he had long forgotten her. And everyone knew Jane Shore was all Edward thought about now. There was no further hope for Blanche.

She realised now that she had ruined her life for her greed but it was too late. She felt as much of a prisoner as those wretched creatures covered in grime and gore who were being driven to their deaths for taking part in some insurrection no one seemed to know much about. The King had suddenly ridden pell-mell towards Wales, that was all anyone understood and Jasper Tudor had been at the back of it.

The King must be very disappointed then, for it was clear no Earl of Pembroke had been captured. Was that why he wore that sourly disgruntled face as he rode by, no whit aware that Blanche was there?

He looked very much like a man who was right uneasy about his conscience, however predictably different his brothers appeared to be.

What drew her eyes suddenly to the fettered, helpless prisoners again, she would never know. Some sixth sense that would not, in any circumstances, be denied? No matter what the reason, glance at them afresh she certainly had—and at one in particular who slumped exhausted against the side of the cart, his arms tied cruelly tightly behind his back and his head lolling back and forth with the motion of the vehicle. On that terribly scarred and battered countenance, was the look of a man pushed almost beyond endurance by beatings. He would hardly know where he was or what new atrocities might be waiting for him in the Tower; possibly he was almost past caring. God's head; she knew him. She knew him.

"Robin!" she heard herself scream in a frenzy that burst out of her like an explosion. She couldn't believe it; didn't want to believe it. Not that he could be reduced to this: to Edward's helpless prisoner due to be drawn to his death on hurdles if further tortures did not kill him.

The carts had rattled by and Edward's men had clattered after them. Amidst the cheers, very few people had heard her horrified scream. Those that had merely turned away and shrugged; probably they thought she was demented. She stood there stunned for a moment longer and then she turned and plunged recklessly through the crowds, heading back for Cheape and Master Cartwright's house.

Blanche hardly knew what she was doing, except that she was praying the old mercer would not be at home. He ought not to be for it was not his usual hour. Blanche ran in, ignoring the stares of the servants; she made for her own room.

Straight to the chest of fine clothes standing beneath the window. She wrenched open the lid and sought wildly amongst the gaily coloured silks and brocades for the most becoming of the gowns and the most elaborate tissue head-dress. She dressed with haste then brushed out her shining hair before she coiled it up tightly again under her glistening henin. Pearls for her neck. Perfumed oil stroked into her hands.

I am mad, she thought. Mad. What do I really suppose all this will achieve? Have I not already acknowledged that King Edward wants no more of me? Why should he see me; listen to me? Why, above all, should he listen to my pleas that he should pardon Robin of Wakefield?

She felt tears on her cheeks and she whisked them away with anger; they would spoil her careful paint. Robin, Robin! Never had she thought even to glimpse him again. There was no way she could avoid this masive effort to try to save him. Only she just might have the power. She was compelled to try to use it.

Blanche was sweeping down the stairs; she could smell venison cooking. Cartwright must be almost home; she must hurry.

"Bring round a litter!" she shouted through to the grinning apprentices in the shop. "Hurry!"

"Hey, what's this?" they chaffed her. "Running away from the old man are you?"

"God damn your impudence!" lashed Blanche. "I'll have him whip you all!"

They only laughed harder but they took care to obey her. She was scrambling inside the litter only just in time outside the house, and giving the order to go to Westminster in a trembling voice. Astonished glances greeted her, but the men moved off.

She heard Master Cartwright bustling down the street, shouting.

"Blanche! Blanche, my love, is that you?"

Devil run off with him. She was not going back to him now whatever happened to her. Ever.

In ten minutes they were at the palace and she was alighting, paying the men from the little purse of gold that hung at her wrist. Daring to go forward into the outer courtyard of the palace she had briefly known so well. Since then it had been Warwick's and King Henry's. Now it was Edward's again.

The King's guards were coming forward, eyeing her with lust mixed with suspicion.

"What do you want here, girl?"

She pulled herself up straight as she had once noticed the royal ladies did; it always had an intimidating effect on an audience. She looked them straight in the eye.

"Take care how you address me," said Blanche.

"You must state your business."

"Very well," shortly. "I shall do so. Take me to Jane Shore."

* * *

How pretty this room in the palace was. Blanche had never seen it before with its delicate hangings of rose and gold brocade, its chests carved out of a pale wood that gave a sense of lightness and space to the small apartment. Glorious colours were splashed into the tiled, circular floor space from the stained-glass oriel window. A comfortably cushioned window seat ran the whole length of the window; there was a dainty gold harp standing near to a small and elegant chair.

The supercilious servants had left her alone. Blanche swallowed hard and seated herself on the chair. Nervously she reached out and plucked experimentally at the sweetness of the harp-strings. She could not know if her old acquaintance Mistress Shore would want to bother with her. Jane might sense an attempt at rivalry and she was far too astute to jeopardise her own sway over the King.

The swish of expensive skirts suddenly made Blanche turn round. She had leapt to her feet ready to go and greet Jane with enthusiasm, but when she realised who had in fact come into the room, she stood wide-eyed and foolish, her heart sinking. Then fell humbly to her knees.

Queen Elizabeth was eyeing her curiously, analytically. She folded her hands very calmly at her bodice, steadily taking in the richness of Blanche's attire.

"You may rise," she told her. "I suppose I should not be surprised to see you here, mistress."

"Oh but—I asked for Mistress Shore," faltered Blanche. At once she could have bitten her tongue out. But the Queen only shrugged.

"So I understand. That is why I have come. I was most anxious to see what kind of friends she had."

"By your leave, Your Grace, I cannot tell if she would still be my friend or not. But I meant to ask her to beg the King to see me."

Elizabeth Woodville's face hardened. Blanche hastened on.

"For I knew he would never trouble himself with me

otherwise, madame! And how would such as I dare to sue kindness of you? I am a wretched creature."

"What do you want of the King?" Elizabeth demanded with asperity.

"Madame, mercy. Mercy for one whom we—both—betrayed. Nothing else, I swear it."

The Queen was visibly relenting. There was actually a sparkle of interest.

"Now I see the truth of it! Robin of Wakefield."

"Your Grace, help him! You know why he left my lord the King—and it was my fault! He has somehow offended the King's grace deeply in a way I cannot understand, I saw him being dragged to the Tower. Oh believe me, madame, he would never have left King Edward but for me!"

Elizabeth turned away. She looked crestfallen.

"I will tell you," she said quietly, "I grieved for him too. He was a kind man. But he has been a traitor, mistress. I cannot tell you more. His sin is grave."

"Can it be so grave that the King can in no way forgive?" pleaded Blanche in desperation. "He knows Robin. He must know he should not die in chains!"

The Queen sighed, frowning.

"Suppose I were to help you—if I could? Ah no"—as Blanche would have hurled herself in gratitude at her feet again—"you ought not to count on it. And I confess myself puzzled why I should wish to show you favour. The King has used you. But I believe my contempt for Jane Shore now overrides my memories and I deeply regret any hurt to Robin of Wakefield. Mistress, if he is freed, what can you do for him? Take him away? Swear to show your face no more at my husband's court?"

"Lady," faintly, "how could I promise? How do I know

he would not smite me down? Once I feared him greatly."

"And now?"

"Let him kill me if he wishes it," miserably. "So long as he goes free."

The Queen said no more, only turned and went away.

* * *

Robin, lying on his foul straw mattress in the Tower, thought the guards had come to drag him away to the torture chamber, or even to death. He struggled up weakly, finding himself seized and propelled urgently out into the echoing passages beyond, and then, startlingly, out of a massive barred door and into the fresh, fiercely welcome daylight. The river flowed past almost at his feet and a covered barge in which sat several of Edward's pikemen, awaited him.

"Where do you take me?" he kept asking, but no one would answer.

The oarsmen picked up the blades and with a steady beat on the water, the barge went off towards the stairs at Westminster. Before they reached their destination, a hood had been placed over Robin's head.

His protests were silenced angrily.

"The King's orders. You are not to be seen, my lord, entering the palace."

And he was to see nothing himself. Only feel himself steered with the same urgency up the water steps and into the precincts of Westminster. More corridors awaited him, more stairs. At last he sensed himself in a large presence chamber, where many people tramped about. Someone shouted and the place was cleared of the rustle of skirts and the stamp of feet.

"You are to be left alone," said his guides at this point.

The discomfort of standing here, blind, prickling with unease, was enormous. At any moment, Robin felt sure someone was to spring on him from behind with a dagger. Then, abruptly, his attention was diverted. He could hear approaching voices; they were raised and argumentative. He remembered them well—King Edward's and the Queen's.

"Do you know what you are asking?" the King was growling now. Surely the royal pair stood in the doorway, staring at their hooded captive. "You know what he has done!"

"I pity him," the Queen reiterated stubbornly. "And even that whore, God help me."

"You grow very soft, wife," said Edward jeeringly but he was coming forward to stand in front of Robin, and despite himself compassion was beginning to bedevil him. That was the trouble: Elizabeth was right. Had the King not meddled with Robin's woman likely none of this furore might have ensued. Certainly the Countess Margaret would never have been plucked from obscurity to add her menace to Lancaster.

"Wakefield," he said at last, "you will understand that you have friends amongst the women."

"I ever expected that of my lady the Queen," replied Robin hoarsely. "And in all that I have done, I would never have hurt her."

"But me?" grated Edward.

"I hate you no longer, my liege. My quarrel is done."

"You see!" cried Elizabeth triumphantly. "It is as I told you, my lord. Have mercy for this man!"

Edward grunted in a surly fashion.

"I am making a condition," he told Robin gruffly.

"My liege, I beg you, let me take off this hood. I am fair smothered."

"Not yet!"

Robin sensed that the King turned and snapped his fingers at someone to bid them come into the apartment. A woman! it had to be by the rustle of silken skirts and the waft of perfume. Holy Cross, didn't he know that scent of old? Was it not the one he had never thought to smell again?

He was beginning to tremble, to sweat. It wasn't possible. Not even Edward would dare.

"You know, don't you?" challenged the King. "Before you speak another word, I warn you that this is my condition. Take this woman off my hands and away from court and you can have your freedom."

"No!" roared Robin furiously, beginning to tear at the hood with both hands. "No, God damn it, why should I? Never I say! Never!"

Blanche burst into tears. She ran to him and ripped the hood from his head, not caring for what Edward might say.

"Accept, Robin!" she pleaded desperately through a welter of tears. "Accept, in God's name! You can cast me from you if you wish, but at least use me to save your life!"

For a moment he refused even to look at her but suddenly he felt forced to turn his head. He had loved her so much before Margaret, thought her the fairest of women. Sheer curiosity prompted him to look on her again. He caught his breath; lovely she still was. A little plumper perhaps but it suited her. She looked different in so many ways: as though the past year had changed her as it had belaboured him. Odd. Whoever might have dreamed he would start to soften towards her, to actually pity her, when it was his life at stake?

"He will take me, my lord!" Blanche was crying out in a frenzy of appeal to Edward. "He will, I swear it! I beg you to spare him!"

Edward retorted: "I have not yet heard him speak. And he was not ever wont to be afraid of me."

Robin found himself straightening and staring at Edward with sudden implacability. Blanche had seized hold of his arm with tight, imploring fingers. The first instinct had been to throw her off with violence, but he did not do that.

"I am still not afraid to speak to you, Sire."

"Do you accept the terms of your freedom? Or have you been meddling so high of late that this lady is too common for your taste?"

"No!" Robin was angry now. "Put by your sneering, my lord!"

"Ay, well, the lady's laid in grave, I suppose. Your chance is flown."

Blanche had stopped crying. Instead she was watching Robin, her face very pale. Lady? What was it that she did not know? Maybe would never know if Robin chose not to tell her?

"Chance?" bitterly. "You choose to misunderstand my motives, my liege. Too many ambitious friends surround you, I never was one of them. Let us have done with this, Sire. I'll speak plainly. Madman I may be, but I will accept your terms. The woman shall leave Westminster with me."

The Queen had cried out with delight, clapping her hands together. After one wildly disbelieving, but marvelling look, Blanche la Belle had thrown her arms around Robin and clung to him as though she would never let him go again.

"God's mercy!" she was whispering then, over and over.

"I do not deserve it! I do not!"

Robin felt bemused. But curiously the whole of his anger against her was gone, just as Margaret Wynford was. He found himself sighing a little wearily but then, before the King and Queen, he put both arms around her and kissed her tear-stained face.

"Enough of misery," he told her quietly. "Enough now, Blanche."

* * *

Queen Elizabeth watched them leave the palace together. They left the courtyard and went beyond to embark on the river. Where would he take her? Back to Wakefield? Would he indeed keep her under his protection? Marry her? Surely there must be a chance for them; they had loved each other once and they were still young.

The Queen sighed, and went away from the window.

One day Robin would doubtless tell Blanche about Margaret Wynford. By then, for both their sakes, Elizabeth Woodville hoped the pain of Wakefield's astonishing memories would long have eased, and that they would have taken eagerly the opportunity she had striven to give them, and learned to love again.

THE END